SPECIAL MESSAGE TO READERS

THE ULVERSCROFT FOUNDATION
(registered UK charity number 264873)
was established in 1972 to provide funds for research, diagnosis and treatment of eye diseases. Examples of major projects funded by the Ulverscroft Foundation are:-

- The Children's Eye Unit at Moorfields Eye Hospital, London
- The Ulverscroft Children's Eye Unit at Great Ormond Street Hospital for Sick Children
- Funding research into eye diseases and treatment at the Department of Ophthalmology, University of Leicester
- The Ulverscroft Vision Research Group, Institute of Child Health
- Twin operating theatres at the Western Ophthalmic Hospital, London
- The Chair of Ophthalmology at the Royal Australian College of Ophthalmologists

You can help further the work of the Foundation by making a donation or leaving a legacy. Every contribution is gratefully received. If you would like to help support the Foundation or require further information, please contact:

THE ULVERSCROFT FOUNDATION
The Green, Bradgate Road, Anstey
Leicester LE7 7FU, England
Tel: (0116) 236 4325

website: www.foundation.ulverscroft.com

THE SHAPE OF SUMMER

When Anna Blakeney is offered the temporary job of looking after the Chatham children, Sara and Jeremy, her guilty feelings about the deaths of their parents in the car which Anna's father was driving make it impossible for her to refuse. She instantly dislikes the children's half-brother and guardian, Drewe, but while he is away she reckons she can sort out her problems with her boyfriend Ricky. Then Ricky meets someone new, and Anna is surprised to find that her own passions have changed in the most unpredictable way . . .

BARBARA CUST

THE SHAPE OF SUMMER

Complete and Unabridged

LINFORD
Leicester

First published in Great Britain in 1975 by
Robert Hale & Company
London

First Linford Edition
published 2014
by arrangement with
Robert Hale Limited
London

A catalogue record for this book is available from the British Library.

ISBN 978–1–4448–1971–7

Published by
F. A. Thorpe (Publishing)
Anstey, Leicestershire

Set by Words & Graphics Ltd.
Anstey, Leicestershire
Printed and bound in Great Britain by
T. J. International Ltd., Padstow, Cornwall

This book is printed on acid-free paper

1

The sleek black car drew up outside the hotel, and Anna Blakeney at the reception desk saw a tall, fair man push open the glass doors and advance with a rapid stride. She hesitated, her fingers gripping the edge of the counter convulsively, then took a deep breath as he approached her. It wasn't hard to guess his identity, and she would have given a great deal not to have had to face him but there was no point in running away. Sooner or later they must meet.

He said crisply: 'My name's Chatham. The manageress is expecting me.'

'Will you come this way?' asked Anna. 'Mrs. Brayle will be here in a moment but I am Anna Blakeney. Your father and step-mother were in my parents' car when the accident occurred.'

Drewe Chatham looked at her keenly. 'Can you tell me exactly what happened?'

'Mr. and Mrs. Chatham were staying here with Sara and Jeremy and as I'm the receptionist I saw a good deal of them. My mother runs — ran — a small pottery, and because Mrs. Chatham was interested in it she and your father became very friendly with my parents. A couple of days ago a minor fault developed in your father's car and he had to leave it in a garage at Polcaster. He mentioned this in the pottery, and as he'd arranged to pick it up yesterday my parents offered him and his wife a lift into Polcaster. It had been raining heavily, my father's car skidded on the hill leading out of St. Aurryns and collided with a stone wall. All — all four of the passengers were killed.'

'And Sara and Jeremy?'

'They'd stayed behind to go surfing with me. It was my day off, and we were all down on the beach when the police rang through.'

Anna's hands clenched. To the end of her life she would never forget the exhilaration of riding the waves that sunny morning, Jeremy's happy shouts, and the sudden appearance of the hall porter frantically beckoning them in. There was no question of breaking things gently. He'd blurted the tragic news straight out because Sara had to supply her stepbrother's address so that the police could communicate with him immediately.

Anna thought the man facing her showed remarkably little emotion. His grey eyes were cool and appraising, and his feelings completely under control. If he were upset by the death of his father he certainly didn't show it, and she resented that.

'How have Sara and Jeremy taken it?' he asked.

'Naturally they're very upset, but Sara's more bitter about it than Jeremy. He's completely stunned, but then he's much younger.'

'Yes. Where are they now?'

'The Vicar's wife has taken them today. Sara would have preferred to stay here, but Jeremy wouldn't go without her. It seemed better to get him out of the way with so much coming and going. The — the inquest is fixed for tomorrow.'

'I'd better see the police and the hospital authorities. There will be arrangements to make. I take it you can put me up here tonight?'

'Oh yes, for as long as you like.'

The door opened and Mrs. Brayle came in, her face controlled but her distress reflected in her eyes.

'Mr. Chatham, may I extend my deepest sympathy.'

'Thank you,' he answered formally.

Anna rose to her feet. 'I'll get back to the desk,' she said and thankfully escaped.

She was attending to one of the other guests when Drewe Chatham strode through the foyer a few minutes later, and soon afterwards Mrs. Brayle came to relieve her while she took her afternoon break.

'I never meant you to be the one to tell Mr. Chatham the details,' said the manageress. 'You should have called me.'

'It didn't matter,' said Anna wearily. 'Nothing matters now. If only I'd made sure that Daddy had had that new tyre fitted.'

'You can't possibly blame yourself for that,' said Mrs. Brayle vigorously. 'You noticed that tyre was wearing, and you told your father so. He promised to have a new one fitted last week so it wasn't your fault that he didn't keep his word.'

'But I should have checked. I knew how he put things off.'

Nothing could have altered Stephen Blakeney or quenched his eternal optimism and he was content with very little so long as he could scratch a sufficient living from free-lance journalism. So far he'd managed by writing country articles for the dwindling number of magazines which would accept them, but Anna had wondered how much longer it could last. The pottery helped but its profits were very small, and if it hadn't been for her salary as receptionist at the Ocean Hotel they couldn't have afforded to run the shabby shooting-brake and have enough left over to pay for her father's tobacco and her mother's expensive art magazines.

That was why Anna hadn't left home when she'd finished the training course for hotel receptionists. She'd wanted to go abroad or at least to London where she could gain experience, but without her to keep an eye on them her parents would have been quite lost. They were both impractical, spending money when it was available and doing without things when it wasn't, and she had to make sure that they were paying their bills and eating sensibly. Her father had always hated town life and when he married her mother, straight from art school and as happy go lucky as himself, they'd found the cottage in Cornwall, buying it with money advanced by her mother's father.

They'd settled blissfully there, and during Anna's childhood things hadn't been too bad because until his death when she was seventeen her grandfather had always come to the rescue. When he died six years ago he left her five hundred pounds, and she'd used part of it to pay her fees and travelling expenses for her training. She'd known that she'd have to get a job near home, and hotel work was the only opportunity which offered any prospect of earning a decent living.

In the beginning her ambition was to run an hotel of her own one day, but that had faded since she'd realised her feeling for Ricky Beeston. He was bound up now with her future happiness, but Ricky was tied to his mother as she was tied to her parents and nothing could be resolved until Mrs. Beeston died. That wasn't as callous as it sounded. Her heart had been weak for years, and she herself had commented that she couldn't expect to make old bones. It seemed ironical that she should still be living while Anna's parents had been snuffed out, all in an instant.

'Have you decided what you're going to do yet?' asked Mrs. Brayle hesitantly. 'I don't want to lose you and you could come to live in the hotel if you don't want to stay on at the cottage. It would make a nice little nest egg for you if you sold it.'

'Yes, but I don't intend to do anything in a hurry.'

'That's sensible,' agreed Mrs. Brayle. 'Why don't you go out for a while? It's a lovely day; far too good to spend in here.'

'I'll walk to the Vicarage and find out how Sara and Jeremy are going on. Is Mr. Chatham expected back for dinner?'

'Yes, he'd said he'd see them then.'

'I should have thought he'd have wanted to see them right away.'

'So should I but perhaps he's never been very close to them. It could have been a great shock to him when his father married again, and I don't imagine he and his stepmother had anything in common,' said Mrs. Brayle shrewdly. 'That dolly prettiness and those baby ways wouldn't appeal to his type.'

'Perhaps not,' said Anna, not much interested in Mr. Chatham. She'd summed him up as cold and egotistical, and wasn't sorry to think that he would soon be going back to London.

At the Vicarage Jeremy Chatham was mowing the lawn while his sister was sprawled moodily on a garden seat. She was a leggy blonde of seventeen with a curtain of hair which almost hid her blue eyes and remarkably pretty features. Jeremy was tall for ten but angular with it, and his expression was perpetually half-anxious as if he were afraid of offending people. From what she'd seen of the family Anna guessed that

Sara had been her father's darling, and Jeremy, the second son and only averagely bright, had had to struggle to keep up with her. Anna liked him much better than his sister, however, and now when she smiled at him he immediately beamed back at her.

'Do you think it's awful of me to be mowing the lawn?' he enquired, 'only there's nothing else to do and it did need it so badly.'

'It isn't the thing at a time like this,' said Sara flatly, but Anna answered reassuringly: 'It seems to me sensible to occupy yourself. It's what your mother and father would have wished.'

Sara shrugged, and Anna went on quickly: 'Your brother has arrived at the hotel. He's gone into Polcaster, but he'll be back for dinner.'

Sara shrugged again. 'And then I suppose he'll take us back to Heathlands and dump us there with Mrs. Mabledon.'

'She's the housekeeper,' explained Jeremy, 'and she's quite nice really, not like Mummy and Daddy of course but — '

He gulped, and with his head down began to push the mower harder than ever.

Sara said bitterly: 'It was going to be such a wonderful summer now that I'd left school. Daddy said I needn't settle down to a job right away, not unless I wanted to — '

She hunched herself up on the seat, and Anna said sympathetically: 'Had you some career in mind for later on?'

'I was looking forward to some freedom, to travelling about and enjoying myself. This holiday in Cornwall was to be only the beginning.'

Instead it proved to be the end, thought Anna, and said aloud: 'Well, I'll see you both later.'

Jeremy gazed at her appealingly, but she hardened her heart. She knew that if she gave him the slightest encouragement he would ask to come with her, and she wanted to be alone for a while. There was only one person's company she would have welcomed at the moment, and he wasn't available. Ricky Beeston had been in London for the past two days and he wasn't due back until tonight. When he did return and learned what had happened he would be over to see her right away, and she longed desperately for the feel of his arms round her. She'd known Ricky all her life, but it wasn't until they were both grown up that they'd realised how much they had in common.

It was surprising in a way that they'd fallen for each other when they'd been brought up so differently. There had never been much money in the Blakeney family whereas at Welling Manor Ricky had lived a life of comparative luxury as the only son of a doting mother, his father having died when he was quite small. When he left school his mother couldn't bear the thought of his going away to follow a career so she'd set him up in an antique shop in Polcaster, and since he got on well with people and could afford to pay an assistant to deal with the humdrum side of the work he enjoyed the life. In spite of the fact that his mother suffered from a weak heart she liked to entertain, and that was how he and Anna had developed their acquaintanceship into something much deeper.

There'd been a crisis in the kitchen at the Manor just before a dinner party, and the Ocean Hotel had been implored to help out. Anna had driven herself to the Manor with one of the chef's special strawberry meringues and Ricky had taken it from her with his endearing three-cornered smile, saying: 'How good of you to come to our rescue. The cook slipped in some spilled fat, spraining her ankle badly, and the dinner guests are already here.'

'What about the rest of the dinner?' enquired Anna.

'Fortunately the main course was already prepared so my mother has put it in the oven and she and I will dish up and serve the meal.'

'Couldn't I help? It's not very easy to

cope with guests if you're constantly dashing in and out of the kitchen?'

'If you're sure you don't mind it would be wonderful,' said Ricky gratefully, and that was the beginning.

He insisted on taking Anna out to dinner to compensate her for sacrificing her evening, and soon they were spending more and more time together. She found herself falling in love with him and his ardent kisses signified that he was anything but indifferent to her, but his mother was always there in the background and Anna sensed that Mrs. Beeston in spite of her charming manners didn't think she was good enough for her son. She was the last person Anna could have opened her heart to and sometimes the girl wondered despondently how it would all end, but Ricky said optimistically that his mother would come round eventually if only they were patient.

So Anna had had no one to whom she could pour out her grief and sorrow, and she longed for Ricky to come home and comfort her. She walked steadily on, trying to make some plans for the future, hardly daring to anticipate that now she was alone in the world Ricky would urge her to marry him as soon as possible.

Finally, tired out both physically and mentally, she made her way back to the hotel, to discover when she went to the staff table in the dining-room that Drewe Chatham had returned from Polcaster and that Sara and Jeremy had joined him for dinner. Anna ate her meal quickly so that she could relieve Mrs. Brayle at the reception desk, and as she was entering up accounts in the ledger during a quiet spell Drewe Chatham came out of the lounge and walked towards her.

'Can you spare me a few moments this evening?' he asked abruptly, 'or are you on duty until late?'

'I was off this afternoon so I'm on until eleven tonight, I'm afraid,' Anna told him.

He frowned. 'Then we'll have to talk

here. It's about Sara and Jeremy. I must go back to London tomorrow, but I'd prefer them to stay on here for a day or two until I can fix something up.'

'Well, we are fairly full, but I'm sure Mrs. Brayle would manage to accommodate them. If they wouldn't mind changing their rooms I know we have some vacancies on the top floor until the end of the week.'

'Would you be willing to keep your eye on them? Jeremy seems to have taken a fancy to you.' Drewe Chatham sounded as if he couldn't understand his stepbrother's poor taste and Anna felt a prickle of resentment as he went on: 'Of course I would compensate Mrs. Brayle for the loss of your services and it would only be for a short while.'

'I'd be happy to do what I could,' said Anna stiffly, and then her generous nature triumphed over her dislike of his manner. 'I'd do anything to help Jeremy because he seems so vulnerable. I don't mean that Sara hasn't felt the death of her parents, but his whole world has collapsed.'

'That's why I'm anxious he should be down here when the funeral takes place and Sara too. After that it's merely a question of expediting my own marriage so that my fiancée can take charge of Sara and Jeremy. I shall be leaving here immediately after the inquest tomorrow so may I have my bill tonight?'

'Certainly,' said Anna, trying to hide her astonishment as he walked away. She wondered what kind of girl was willing to take on such a self-sufficient man though possibly he showed a different side of his nature to her. For Jeremy's sake it was to be hoped that the future Mrs. Chatham was more human than her prospective husband.

Sara didn't disguise her annoyance at being left at the Ocean Hotel, and said that it was mean of Drewe not to have taken her back to London with him.

'It isn't so bad here,' ventured Jeremy, and she turned on him roundly.

'Not so bad for you perhaps because you like poking round the rocks and the seashore, but what is there for me to do? It was different when Daddy was running us about in the car; now I'm bored rigid. Besides, I'm grown-up, and Drewe has no right to keep me down here like a child. If he didn't want to leave me alone in his flat I could have stayed with Althea.'

'She might not have wanted you,' said Jeremy shrewdly. 'I don't think she likes us much.'

Sara went red. 'Nonsense. You're only a scruffy schoolboy so you can't expect her to be interested in you, but I get on well with her and when she's married to Drewe she's bound to introduce me to lots of people.'

'I don't think she will,' persisted Jeremy, 'and I wish she wasn't going to marry Drewe.'

'Well, she is so you'll have to make the best of it.'

So Mr. Chatham's fiancée was called Althea and Jeremy didn't care for her.

Anna hoped that he would change his mind when he was living in the same house as his brother's wife otherwise it wouldn't be a very happy prospect. She did her best to make the next few days as relaxed as possible for him, and was rewarded by the fact that his face lost some of its anxious lines and he was sleeping better.

That was the only bright spot, however, in her present existence. Ricky was back home and had supported her through the ordeal of the inquest with its verdict of 'Death from Misadventure', but he hadn't mentioned marriage. He'd asked her rather awkwardly what her plans were, and when she said that she'd not yet made up her mind what to do he'd murmured that it would be silly to decide anything in a hurry and that since she could stay on at the hotel she could afford to let matters drift for a while.

She was sure that Mrs. Beeston was at the back of all this, but it was a blow that Ricky hadn't forced the issue once and for all. She knew that he was loath to upset his mother on account of her weak heart, but surely he didn't intend to allow her to run his life completely. In bed at night Anna tossed restlessly while the hollows sharpened under her cheekbones so that her deep blue eyes looked enormous in her face, and the cloud of dark hair seemed too weighty for her slender neck.

In London Drewe Chatham was also finding that his plans were going awry. He hadn't expected Althea Lymington to be overjoyed at the prospect of a hasty wedding and a quick move to the country to take charge of his stepbrother and stepsister, but he'd thought that she would acknowledge it to be the only solution to his predicament. He definitely hadn't anticipated that she would shake her head decisively, refusing flatly to marry him by licence.

'It isn't on, Drewe,' she said coolly. 'I certainly couldn't be ready to marry you at a moment's notice, and anyway I don't want a hole and corner affair with all kinds of rumours flying around. I'd hate that and so would Daddy. Also I haven't had a chance to tell you this but he's flying to the States in a fortnight's time and since he's anxious to look up his business interests in Australia in the near future he's thinking of making a round trip. He's asked me to go with him so you wouldn't expect me to forgo that, would you, darling?'

Her voice took on a coaxing note as she smiled confidently at him.

'No, not at any other time, but I really am in a spot, Althea. I must be in Brussels next week to negotiate that contract and I can't dump Sara and Jeremy at Heathlands, then leave them to their own devices.'

'There's Mrs. Mabledon in the house.'

'She refuses to take the responsibility for them. After all, it is asking a lot to expect her to run the house and look after them as well.'

'Then find someone who will,' said

Althea carelessly. 'You can always get people if you pay enough.'

'It's not quite as easy as that,' said Drewe. He put his hands on her shoulders and pulled her gently towards him. 'Sweet, won't you sacrifice your world tour and make a home for Sara and more particularly Jeremy? He's very unhappy and bewildered, and he needs some stability in his life for the next year or two. I know I'm asking a lot of you, but I'll make it up to you later on.'

'Drewe, once we're married and involved with a home and a family there won't be the opportunity for world tours, that's why I must seize it now. After all, Sara and Jeremy aren't babies. It's only a question of someone keeping an eye on them, and I'm sure there are plenty of people willing to do that. Why don't you put an advertisement in *The Times?*'

Drewe's hands fell to his sides. 'If that's your last word then naturally I must take further steps.'

'I'll ask around,' promised Althea. 'Daddy might hear of someone suitable. Darling, can't you sit down and relax for a moment? We've had very little time together lately, and we're soon to be separated again. I wanted you to take me to that charity concert on Saturday.'

'Sorry, but I've such a lot to arrange that I don't think it will be possible.'

'Well, try, Drewe. Give me a ring on Saturday morning. I shan't be going out before lunch.'

'Very well.'

Drewe kissed her and left the house, driving himself back to the tiny service flat he used as a base in London. When he arrived there he sank wearily into a chair and tried to map out his best course of action. He'd hoped very much that Althea would see things from his point of view and agree to marry him immediately because it would have made matters so much simpler. Now he would have to find a reliable woman to take charge of the household, and he really hadn't time to interview people and take up references.

It was tragic that his father and stepmother should have been killed just when their children needed them so much. His father's second wife had never been able to take the place of his own mother to Drewe but she'd been kind to him, and if he thought she was rather silly and the way his father doted on her was slightly ridiculous he managed not to show it. Sara and Jeremy were only small when he left home and he'd never had much to do with them, but he couldn't evade the responsibility for them now and with a vivid memory of his own grief when his mother died he wanted to assuage their present unhappiness as much as he could.

Her fiancé's suggestion that she should marry him by licence and go down to Heathlands to take care of Sara and Jeremy had given Althea Lymington an unpleasant jolt. She'd met Drewe eight months ago on a ski-ing holiday in Austria and had been attracted to him immediately. She wasn't in love with him because she would always have complete control of her emotions, but he was the type of man she aimed to marry — good looking with an attractive personality and obviously all set to make his way in the business world. Her father was beginning to hint that at twenty-five it was time she was settling down and giving him some grandchildren, and deciding coolly that she might do very much worse than Drewe Chatham she set out to charm him into proposing.

It wasn't difficult for someone with her natural advantages. Her dark hair complemented a pair of huge brown eyes with long curling lashes, and her figure was perfect. She had an adoring father who was almost a millionaire and could deny her nothing, she was an accomplished hostess, and her response to his ardour soon convinced Drewe that here was the perfect wife. They became engaged three months after they met, and were planning an autumn wedding when John and Margaret Chatham were killed.

Althea had been sorry to hear of their deaths of course, but she hadn't realised that she would be affected until Drewe had intimated that he intended to make a home for his stepbrother and sister at Heathlands. Apart from not wanting to be saddled with them. Althea had no intention of living in the country. She and Drewe had talked of buying a house in London in one of the Georgian squares, and Althea had already considered several properties. Heathlands wasn't at all the type of house she visualised as a setting for herself, but on the other hand she didn't want Drewe to bring Sara and Jeremy up to London to live. It would be much better for them to remain at Heathlands with a responsible person in charge. Althea pondered over the problem, and rang Drewe early the next morning.

'Darling, I didn't mean to sound

unsympathetic yesterday,' she said sweetly. 'I do realise what a headache this is for you. Do Sara and Jeremy have to come up to Heathlands now? Couldn't they stay on in Cornwall until you could fix up something for them?'

'The hotel can only keep them a few days longer; their rooms have been booked by other people. As it is they're only staying on because Miss Blakeney has promised to keep her eye on them.'

'Who is Miss Blakeney?'

'She's the receptionist at the hotel and Jeremy has taken a great fancy to her.'

'Then your problem's solved. Offer her more than her present salary to come and take charge at Heathlands until you can make other arrangements. She'll probably jump at the chance. I don't suppose the hotel is paying her all that much.'

'She may not want to leave.'

'You can't know until you tackle her, at any rate it's worth a try.'

'Yes, that's true.'

'Then go to it and good luck,' said Althea gaily.

So to her surprise the next day Anna saw the black car once more nose its way under the hotel portico. Drewe Chatham sprang out and crossed the foyer towards her saying: 'Miss Blakeney, may I have a word with you?'

'Of course, Mr. Chatham. I'm afraid that since we weren't expecting you Sara and Jeremy have gone into Polcaster on the bus.'

'I didn't come to see them but you, and I haven't much time to spare. Would you consider giving up your job here temporarily and coming down to Heathlands to take charge of Sara and Jeremy? The house is on the outskirts of Occambridge in Sussex and about thirty miles from London.'

'But your fiancée — I understood you would be getting married.'

'The wedding can't take place as soon as I'd hoped,' he answered curtly. 'My business is import-export with the headquarters in London and a continental office in Brussels. My father ran the London office and I was in charge in Brussels, but at the moment I'm commuting between the two which presents certain difficulties and means that I will have to spend a good deal of time away from Heathlands. I think it would be best for Sara and Jeremy to go back to their own home but I can't leave them there with only a housekeeper, it wouldn't be fair to her. I need someone whom they trust and like to be with them, and it occurred to me that you would fill the bill.'

'I'm flattered by your confidence in me,' said Anna formally, 'but though I do get on well with Jeremy I can't say the same of Sara. I don't think she would appreciate being under my supervision.'

'I'm not really concerned at the moment with what Sara wants,' said Drewe impatiently. 'She'd resent anyone in authority over her, but she isn't old enough to take charge of the household herself and she must put up with whatever arrangements I make. I want to ensure that Jeremy has a decent home life before he goes back to school, and if I get someone strange in he'll be unhappy and upset. If your conscience is worrying you about deserting Mrs. Brayle I'll make things right with her.'

Anna hesitated. She was tempted to accept his proposition if only to get away from St. Aurryns. Every stone of the place was too bound up with memories for her to be happy there, particularly as Ricky had remained unresponsive, and a change of scene would help to turn her thoughts in a different direction. At the same time if she went away Ricky might realise how much he was missing her and be impelled to take definite action.

On the other hand if she went down to Heathlands she would certainly come into contact with this man every now and again, a prospect which didn't appeal in the least to her. The more she saw of Drewe Chatham the more arrogant and unfeeling she thought him, and she hadn't the slightest desire to form part of his household. She would have liked to help Jeremy, but if it couldn't be done without taking his stepbrother as her employer then she would have to harden her heart.

So now she shook her head decisively. 'I'm sorry, Mr. Chatham, but I can't accept your offer. I don't feel qualified to run your house; I'm sure you need someone with far more experience than I have.'

'I see. I can't persuade you to change your mind?'

'No, I'm afraid not.'

Afterwards Anna was to wonder if Drewe Chatham would have accepted her refusal if Jeremy hadn't come bounding into the hotel at that moment.

'Anna,' he cried, 'look what I bought in the market. Oh, Drewe — ' He stopped short and an anxious frown creased his brow. 'You haven't come to take us away today, have you?'

'No, you won't be returning to Heathlands until Thursday.'

'Who will be there?' asked Jeremy tentatively. 'Just Mrs. Mabledon?'

'No, I have to find someone to look after you properly.'

'I wish it could be Anna,' said Jeremy simply.

Drewe Chatham raised one eyebrow. 'You see?' Then as Anna didn't reply he said an utterly unforgivable thing. 'I understand it was your father who was driving the car.'

Anna went very white, and hated him because he'd touched her in her most vulnerable spot. She knew that it was quixotic to blame herself for not making sure that her father had had a new tyre fitted to the car, but the fact remained that she did. She'd impressed on him that the tyre was badly worn but she should have made sure he did something about it, not allowed him to forget it because his mind was taken up with the article he was drafting. She'd been too busy to drive the car herself for the past week, but she ought to have insisted that he didn't drive it either until it was in order. As a result she felt partly responsible for what had happened, and guilt surged up in her anew when Drewe Chatham spoke.

His eyes narrowed as he saw he'd made an impression, and he followed up his advantage.

'It would only be for a short time and it would be very much in the interests of Jeremy and Sara.'

Jeremy looked from one to the other of them. 'What are you talking about?'

'I was asking Miss Blakeney if she'd agree to coming down to Heathlands to take charge of the house until I'm back in England long enough to make some permanent arrangements.'

'You will say yes, won't you, Anna? It would be super to have you down there. You could coach me in tennis, and we could swim in the pool. It would make all the difference to the rest of the holidays.'

'But I couldn't let Mrs. Brayle down,'

began Anna weakly, and Drewe Chatham interrupted her with: 'I've told you you've no need to worry about that. I'll make things right with her.'

Anna's heart and conscience wouldn't let her protest any further, and by the time Drewe Chatham left again for London everything had been settled. Mrs. Brayle was most understanding, and when she and Anna were alone together she said: 'I don't want to lose you, but I think in this case you're doing the right thing. Get away from here for a while into another atmosphere. Don't worry about the cottage; I think the Knights would take it furnished for a couple of months if you wanted to let it. They were asking me if I knew of anywhere round here to rent as they'd like to stay on at St. Aurryns for a while. They're thinking of settling down in Cornwall now that he's retired, but they want to try it out before buying a property.'

'Perhaps I could do that. I'd rather not leave myself without a home until

I've made some long-term plans for the future.'

'Well, there'll always be a room here for you whenever you feel like a break, and you can come back as receptionist when you've finished at Heathlands if you don't get a better offer.'

'Thank you for everything,' said Anna gratefully. 'I'll be back. I don't intend to lose touch.'

The next three days were a mad whirl but she was glad not to have time to think. She rang Ricky to tell him that she was going away, and he was plainly taken aback.

'Why so soon?' he protested. 'Look, I know we haven't seen much of each other lately, but Mother's not been well and hasn't wanted me to leave her.'

I'm sure she hasn't, thought Anna dryly. She intended to make sure that you wouldn't have the chance to comfort me. Aloud she said: 'I need to get away from here for a while and see things in perspective. For the time being I'm letting the cottage furnished to some people who are staying at the hotel but who want a place of their own temporarily. They won't be using the pottery so I can store my personal belongings there.'

'Give me your new address and telephone number,' demanded Ricky. 'Oh, hell, I wish things weren't so difficult. I'll be in touch.'

The journey down to Sussex was uneventful. Drewe Chatham's powerful car ate up the miles and they arrived at Heathlands in the early evening. Anna was too tired to take in more than a vague impression of a white house with green shutters, and only registered thankfully that Mrs. Mabledon, the housekeeper, was grey-haired and friendly.

'You must all be in need of a meal,' she said, 'but since I didn't know exactly what time you would arrive I put a chicken casserole in the oven. It's all ready now. Would you like to go up to your room first, Miss Blakeney?'

'Sara will take you up,' said her step-brother, and Mrs. Mabledon added: 'It's the room on the right at the top of the stairs, Sara.'

Sara ran lightly up the stairs and Anna followed her.

'There you are,' said the girl carelessly, pushing open the door. 'If you want anything just shout. Jeremy's next door and I'm at the end,' and she disappeared into her own room.

Anna's room was decorated in pale blue and white with wide windows looking out over a rose garden, but she felt a pang of homesickness for her shabby bedroom at the cottage with its faded chintz curtains and bedcover. Here the carpet was thick and built-in clothes cupboards lined one wall, but she would have given all she possessed to be back in St. Aurryns with her father and mother alive and well. Then she pulled herself together, tidied her hair, washed her hands in the adjoining primrose bathroom, and went down to the dining-room.

The chicken casserole was delicious and it was followed by an equally tempting apricot flan, but Anna had to force herself to eat. It wasn't a very comfortable meal since Drewe Chatham was obviously anxious to get it over and start for London while Sara pushed her food round her plate in a bored fashion. Jeremy kept casting troubled looks at Anna until she smiled reassuringly back at him whereupon he began to eat with real appetite.

Drewe Chatham said abruptly: 'I shall be in London for the next couple of days so if there's anything you want to know you can ring me at my flat in the evening. I shan't be able to come down here again before I leave for Brussels, but you should be able to manage. I've opened an account for you at the bank, and you can draw on it for anything within reason. Mrs. Mabledon deals with the tradesmen, and the household bills are paid monthly. I shall be back here in three weeks, and I don't anticipate any desperate crises in that time.'

'Neither do I,' said Anna, 'but if I should need to get in touch with you in a hurry — ?'

'My secretary will know where I am. Here's the office address and telephone number. Anything else?'

'I don't think so.'

'Then I'll be off. Goodbye, Miss Blakeney. Don't forget you're the man of the house now, Jeremy. Sara, while I'm away you might be giving some thought to the kind of career you'd like to take up.'

The black car shot down the drive, and Mrs. Mabledon said: 'Mr. Chatham will wear himself out the way he's going on. Now, Miss Blakeney, would you like to see over the house?'

'Very much,' said Anna, and was taken on a conducted tour, starting at the kitchen, which was a model of stream-lining together with all the latest gadgets, and ending in the drawing-room which had long windows opening out onto a paved terrace.

'It's a beautiful house,' she said warmly, and Mrs. Mabledon nodded.

'Mr. Chatham bought it when he married his second wife, and he was constantly making alterations and improvements. He had the tennis court laid out and then two years ago the swimming pool was constructed especially for the children. It's a real family house.'

'Have you been here a long time?'

'I came when Jeremy was a baby, and I've been very happy working here. I little thought when they all drove away three weeks ago that I'd never see Mr. and Mrs. Chatham again.'

She shook her head sadly, and Anna said impulsively: 'I'll need your help in running the household, Mrs. Mabledon. You know so much more about Sara and Jeremy than I do.'

'You'll not have any trouble with Jeremy. He's an affectionate boy and he's certainly taken to you, but Sara's a different matter. She was her father's girl, and she hasn't much time for women. Still, you're not so much older than her yourself so maybe you'll have some influence on her. She shouldn't be allowed to fritter her life away. It isn't good for anyone to be idle.'

'Well, I'll do my best,' declared Anna, but she sounded more valiant than she really felt. She hadn't much hope of getting close to Sara; she suspected the other girl despised her.

The next morning the sun was shining and her spirits lifted as she dressed and went down to breakfast. Jeremy was already there eating cornflakes, and he said eagerly: 'Can we swim in the pool this morning? It's awfully warm already.'

'We'll see a little later on,' promised Anna, and then helping herself to iced fruit juice she picked up *The Times* which was lying beside her plate. Turning to the back page her eyes idly scanned the columns, then suddenly a name leaped out at her and she read the announcement beneath it.

It didn't seem possible but it was true. Ricky's mother was dead. Anna was filled with remorse for misjudging her, but above all she was conscious of bitter regret. If only she hadn't left St. Aurryns so precipitately, if only she'd been there now to console Ricky who knew what might have happened?

2

Her heart full of sympathy for him, Anna went immediately to the telephone to ring Ricky, and when he answered she burst out: 'Ricky, this is Anna. I've just seen the announcement in *The Times*. I'm so very sorry.'

'Yes,' he said soberly, 'although I've known for years that her heart was weak it was still a great shock. The funeral will take place on Monday. Is there any hope of your being able to come down for it?'

'I'm afraid not,' Anna told him regretfully. 'Mr. Chatham is in London and I can hardly leave Sara and Jeremy so soon, much as I'd like to be with you.'

'It would mean a lot to me to have you here, but I understand how you're placed.'

'What will you do now?' asked Anna tentatively.

'There's been so much to arrange that I haven't had time to consider the future yet. Of course Mother would have wanted me to stay on at the Manor, but the cost of keeping it up increases every year and it's so difficult to get domestic help. The solicitor's coming shortly to talk over the provisions of the will so I shall be in a better position then to decide what to do. Will you be in tomorrow evening if I ring you?'

'Tomorrow evening and every other evening for the next three weeks as far as I can see. Goodbye, Ricky.'

And all my love, she longed to add, but held it back. If Ricky wanted to stay on at Welland Manor how gladly she would marry him and help him to run it, but that was something he would have to decide for himself.

Sara had drifted down to the dining-room and was drinking black coffee, refusing toast with a shudder.

'I never eat bread,' she said emphatically. 'Do you know how many calories there are in one slice?'

'No, and I don't want to,' retorted Mrs. Mabledon who was clearing the table. 'If you've finished, Sara, then the woman can hoover this room.'

Sara dropped her cup onto the trolley and sauntered out while Anna said: 'Is there anything you want from the shops, Mrs. Mabledon? I'm going into town to get some things I didn't have time to buy in Cornwall. Would you like to come with me, Jeremy?'

'Rather,' he answered, beaming. He wasn't a handsome boy, having rather plain features plentifully sprinkled with freckles, but his grey eyes were wide and well-spaced and he had a heart-warming grin.

'There's nothing I need this morning, thank you, Miss Blakeney, but tomorrow I'll have my weekend list ready. The shopping centre's quite well planned, and there's a car park by the supermarket.'

'I'll show you the way,' promised Jeremy. 'Are you taking Mummy's car?'

To Anna's relief he said it quite calmly since she'd been wondering if it would upset him to see her use his mother's car.

'Yes,' she answered quietly. 'Your stepbrother told me to use it. What about Sara? Do you think she'd like to come too?'

'I'll go and ask her,' volunteered Jeremy, and rushed upstairs.

He came down in a moment to report that Sara didn't want a trip to town, she had plans of her own, so Anna backed the car out of the garage and they set off. Occambridge was a thriving country town, and appeared to cater for most needs. Anna had soon made her purchases, and after paying a visit to the bank to draw some cash suggested elevenses. Jeremy was only too ready to agree, and they found a pleasant café which supplied coffee and chocolate biscuits.

'Sara's silly missing this,' said Jeremy, 'but then girls usually are silly. I mean, she doesn't eat chocolate biscuits or anything really nice because she says they're all fattening. Why does she want to be so thin?'

'It's the fashion,' replied Anna. 'What does Sara most enjoy doing? Does she play tennis? Has she any hobbies?'

'She used to play tennis, but not so much this last year. She likes to swim best. That's really why Daddy had the pool made.'

'Yes, of course, she's an expert swimmer and she took to surfing like a native. She's far better at it than I am, and I've lived in Cornwall all my life.'

'But you're better at walking and doing other things. Can I have this last biscuit?'

'If you're sure it won't spoil your lunch. Mrs. Mabledon will be annoyed if you can't eat that.'

'I'll be hungry again by then,' Jeremy assured her.

The sun shone warmly as they drove back to Heathlands and Sara was already stretched out by the pool, wearing the briefest of scarlet bikinis which enhanced her golden tan. Anna couldn't resist a dip before lunch so she and Jeremy were soon splashing in the water. He was reluctant to come out, and Anna, remembering that she'd heard Mrs. Mabledon mention preparing a salad for lunch, slipped a dress over her swim suit and went into the house to investigate.

'As it's a cold lunch would it inconvenience you if we ate it by the pool?' she enquired tactfully. 'Jeremy and I will carry the dishes out and I'll see that everything's brought back.'

'It makes no difference to me where you eat it,' said Mrs. Mabledon. 'I'm not fond of meals outside myself, but Mrs. Chatham often had hers picnic-fashion in the summer. I'll put the coffee on to percolate, and you can wheel it all down on the big trolley.'

There was a table and chairs down by the pool so the meal was soon set up. Sara, however, made no attempt to help, though she condescended to nibble a salad and drink a glass of iced tomato juice. When they'd finished everything was piled onto the trolley again and Anna, together with Jeremy, prepared to wheel it back to the house.

'It's time Sara did something,' he said indigantly. 'She just lies there and lets everyone else do the work. I think she's lazy.'

Sara turned over onto her stomach. 'Who cares what you think? You're only a little boy.'

'And you're only a stupid girl. You think you look glamorous lying there like that but you don't.'

'That's enough,' said Anna briskly, feeling like a nanny. She wished she could get closer to Sara but the girl held her at arms' length. Naturally she must be missing her mother and it wasn't surprising that she behaved as if she resented Anna, but it did complicate matters. If only, Anna thought, they could find some common ground, but Sara seemed so uninterested in most things.

The next day followed much the same pattern except that Sara disappeared in the afternoon and Jeremy said that she'd probably gone to see friends. Anna acknowledged that she couldn't expect a girl of seventeen to account for every minute of her time, but she wondered how much supervision Mr. Chatham would expect her to exercise. She was still pondering that after dinner when the telephone rang.

'I'll answer it,' and Jeremy rushed into the hall to return in a moment to say: 'It's for you, Anna.'

She knew it could only be Ricky, and her heart began to beat faster.

'Ricky?' she said as she picked up the receiver, and he answered: 'Yes, Anna, it's me.'

'How are you?' she asked, and he gave a queer, strained laugh.

'Bearing up, but only just.'

'What do you mean?'

'I mean that everything's fallen to bits, and there's literally nothing left. Mother had been living on capital for years, and the house is mortgaged up to the roof. She died just in time; in a few months we'd have had to leave the Manor and find rooms in some cheap boarding-house.'

'Then you're penniless?' said Anna blankly.

'When all the debts are cleared I'll have about £500 and that's all.'

'What about the antique shop?'

'That will certainly have to go. It's never paid its way, and £500 won't be enough to inject new life into it. What I can't understand is why Mother didn't tell me what a mess she was in. She must have known for years that the crash was bound to come sooner or later yet she persuaded me to dabble in antiques without any training for a proper career.'

'She didn't want you to leave her,' said Anna slowly. 'Shall you stay on in Cornwall?'

'Heavens, no. I'm never going to be able to earn a living here. As soon as I've sorted things out I shall come up to

London to see what the big city has to offer.'

'Can I help in any way? Have you any friends there?'

'I've a second cousin coming down for the funeral, a woman I've met once or twice, who runs an interior decorating business and is making quite a good thing of it, I believe. She's in her late forties, one of these career women, and I thought I'd ask her if she could put me in the way of anything even if it were only a temporary job.'

'That sounds a good idea,' agreed Anna. 'At least it would give you a chance to look round.'

'That was my idea. However, I mustn't keep you any longer though it's heartening to hear your voice when it's so damned lonely here. I'll ring you again tomorrow night.'

'Let me ring you,' offered Anna quickly. If he were hard up it wasn't fair to expect him to run up a big telephone bill. 'About nineish?'

'Right.'

Anna played Scrabble with Jeremy but her thoughts were on Ricky. It was incredible to think that Mrs. Beeston had lived a life of pretence all these years just to keep her son with her. It was also amazing that he'd never suspected that their finances were dwindling, but then why should he? There'd always seemed to be plenty of money about, and his mother had denied him nothing except the chance of a proper career. Anna's heart ached for him. If only she could have been there to help him dismantle the house. It was no job for a man on his own. She could at least have taken that burden off his shoulders.

She tried not to dwell on her own disappointed hopes. With no money and no job as yet Ricky certainly wasn't in any position to think of marriage even though she would have been willing to live in the tiniest flat and to go on working until he was settled in something congenial. When she rang him the next evening she did her best to sound cheerful and he responded, telling her that Hilary, the second cousin he'd mentioned, had offered him an opening in her business.

Anna said delightedly: 'That is good news, Ricky. Your experience in the antique trade should be useful, and you've always taken an interest in fabrics.'

'True, but Hilary's something of an unknown quantity. I don't really know her very well. She's only paid us a visit from time to time.'

'What about the house? Are you managing to clear that?'

'Yes. Most of the furniture, the pictures and so on, will be sold, and of course the mortgagees are taking over the house itself. Hilary's found me somewhere to live. Two men she knows want a third to share their flat so I've arranged to go in with them. I was wondering if you'd do me a favour, Anna. You mentioned before you left that these tenants of yours at the cottage wouldn't be using the pottery so you were going to store your personal effects there. Would there be room for some things of mine, one or two pieces that I want to keep?'

'Yes, I'm sure they could be fitted in. Mrs. Brayle will give you the key to the pottery. I left it with her.'

'Thanks.'

'How long will it be before you come to London?'

'I shall be up as soon as possible and round to call on you. I take it your employer doesn't object to followers?'

'I shan't ask him. Come as soon as you can, Ricky. I'm longing to see you.'

'It's mutual. 'Bye for now, my sweet.'

She didn't hear from him during the next week, and when she rang him on two different evenings there was no reply. For her the hours after dinner dragged since Jeremy went to bed at nine and Sara shut herself into her room to play pop records. After that first evening she had mooned about the house all day, and far from wondering where she was Anna found herself wishing that Sara would go out more.

'Doesn't Sara have many friends in the neighbourhood?' Anna asked Mrs. Mabledon, and that lady pursed her lips.

'There are the Frenshams, but they're away at the moment. Now that she's left boarding school the friends she made there are scattered.'

'Mr. Chatham mentioned her training for a career, but I can't find out what her interests are.'

'I don't think she knows herself. Her mother spoke of enrolling her for one of those courses in cookery and household management but nothing was settled.'

'I wonder if she'd be interested in hotel work? It has its snags, but at least you're rarely bored and there are opportunities for travel.'

But Sara made it plain that she scorned hotel work. When pressed to say what she would like to do she shrugged and said: 'I wouldn't mind trying some modelling.'

'Why not mention that to your

stepbrother and in the meantime what about language classes or even shorthand and typing? Both can be surprisingly useful in a variety of jobs, and the modelling idea might come to nothing.'

'No, thank you,' said Sara definitely. 'I've only just left school, and I'm certainly not slogging away at classes before I've had five minutes' freedom.'

There Anna had to leave matters, and she foresaw a difficult time before Mr. Chatham returned and could be consulted. Still, Sara was too old to be ordered about so Anna concentrated on Jeremy and had to be content with keeping an unobtrusive eye on his sister. Fortunately the weather continued to be warm and sunny so that they all spent most of their time in the garden and the pool, and Sara's chief ambition seemed to be to acquire a really spectacular tan.

It was on the Wednesday of the following week that Ricky called. Anna was in the garden by herself since friends with a boy of his own age had called to take Jeremy out for the day while Sara had gone into Occambridge to shop, and she ran across the lawn to answer the ring at the door. Her face was alight with pleasure when she recognised her visitor.

'Ricky,' she cried, 'it's lovely to see you,' and he took both her hands in his, smiling down into her eyes.

'Anna, I've missed you.' His glance appraised the drawing-room with its maize-coloured carpet and sea-green silk curtains. 'This is a very nice set-up you've found for yourself.'

'Come into the garden, it's too nice to stay inside, and tell me everything. We'll have tea down by the pool if you can stay.'

'I was hoping you'd ask me.'

'Cross the lawn and turn to your right, then make yourself comfortable while I put the kettle on since Mrs. Mabledon's out. I'll soon join you.'

It took only a few minutes to cut cucumber sandwiches and load the trolley with a tempting selection of cakes. Ricky sprang to his feet as Anna appeared, and said: 'This is wonderful after London. My flat's in Bloomsbury which isn't exactly an ideal spot in this weather.'

'Particularly after Cornwall,' agreed Anna. 'Have you managed to sort everything out?'

'The greater part. There was no point in lingering at St. Aurryns since I had to move out of the house.'

'You haven't started work yet?'

'Not officially. I've been along to look the place over, and Hilary suggested my beginning in earnest at nine o'clock on Monday morning.'

'How do you feel about it?'

He grimaced. 'It's too soon to say, but I've an idea that Hilary won't be the easiest person to work for. Still, I'll have to give the job a fair trial. And what about you? Are you happy here?'

'I'm like you, I haven't really settled down yet. When I read about your mother I wished I'd never left St.

Aurryns. If only I'd been there to help.'

'Yes, it wasn't easy. If I'd known too what was going to happen . . . '

He didn't finish his sentence, but Anna guessed his thoughts.

She said impulsively: 'I'm still the same, Ricky. The fact that you no longer own the Manor doesn't make any difference to me.'

'But it alters everything. I've nothing to offer anyone now, at least not yet.'

'But you soon will have. I believe you'll do very well in interior decorating.'

He lifted her hand and rubbed it against his cheek.

'You're so good for me, Anna. You restore my faith in myself. Now let's stop talking about me for a moment and return to you. Do you intend to remain here for long?'

'I don't quite know. Mr. Chatham didn't specify any period, but he'll expect me to stay at least until Jeremy goes back to school and then there's Sara.'

'How old is she?'

'Almost eighteen, and unfortunately she resents me. At least she keeps me at a distance which makes it impossible for me to help her.'

'Oh well, she'll probably come round before long,' said Ricky easily.

'I hope so. Why, here she is now.'

Ricky rose to his feet as Sara appeared round the corner of the house and sauntered towards them.

'I didn't know you had a visitor,' she said coolly. 'Am I interrupting anything?'

Ricky smiled at her. 'Only my making a pig of myself over these cakes. I forgot to have any lunch today.'

'Ricky, why didn't you tell me?' cried Anna, 'and I'd have provided something more substantial.'

'Not to worry, I shan't fade away.'

'Stay to dinner and then you'll be sure of one good meal,' invited Sara casually. 'Perhaps in the fullness of time Anna will introduce us.'

Anna ignored the rudeness and said

quietly: 'Sara, this is a friend of mine, Ricky Beeston. Ricky, this is Sara Chatham.'

'How do you do, Mr. Beeston. Will you excuse me while I go and change? I intend to swim in the pool; wouldn't you like a dip?'

'Don't mock me,' answered Ricky ruefully. 'It's sheer torture wearing a collar on a day like this.'

'No need to suffer, you can have a pair of Daddy's trunks. Come on.'

She walked towards the house, looking at him over her shoulder, and he hesitated.

'Would you mind, Anna?'

'Why should I?'

'Come on,' called Sara impatiently, and he began to run after her.

It was a relief that Sara hadn't been sulky and unwelcoming, anything was better than that, Anna assured herself, but all the same it was a bit disconcerting to find herself playing gooseberry while Sara and Ricky frolicked in the pool. They were both excellent swimmers, and when they were tired of the water they lay on the tiled verge of the pool and sunbathed.

Sara looked quite different when she was animated. Her blue eyes sparkled against the apricot tan of her skin and her flaxen hair fell in a silky curve to her shoulders. She made no secret of the fact that she found Ricky attractive, and he responded in an amused, indulgent fashion.

He stayed for dinner and it was the pleasantest evening Anna had so far spent at Heathlands. When he finally left Sara said: 'Why don't you come down again on Sunday? Unless you've something better to do, of course.'

Walking down to the gate with him Anna remarked: 'You've made a decided hit there. I've never seen Sara in such a good mood.'

'I thought it might make things easier for you if I played up to her,' responded Ricky, 'and I must admit it wasn't much of a hardship with the pool and that delicious meal laid on.'

'You might as well make the most of it. I don't suppose I shall be here very long.'

'See you on Sunday then, all being well.'

Ricky came down to Heathlands again at the weekend, and Sara exuded charm. If Anna felt a touch of guilt at having him there she salved her conscience by telling herself that it made Sara so much easier to live with. Jeremy hadn't fallen so completely under the newcomer's spell. He was inclined to be wary but Anna suspected a hint of jealousy in his attitude because Ricky was her friend.

The next Sunday the weather turned dull with a chilly wind, and after a brief swim Anna suggested a walk. Ricky agreed, but Sara, who hated walking, refused to go with them and since Jeremy also elected to stay at home Anna and Ricky set out by themselves. She was glad of this since she'd had very little opportunity of getting him to herself, and as they struck off across the heath she said: ‘How are you settling down in your job?’

‘So-so. I find it rather galling being treated as a kind of junior clerk after running my own show. Hilary’s good at her work, but like most career women she’s inclined to be bossy which doesn’t suit me. I’m thinking of making a change.’

‘To what?’

‘What chance is there of an opening in the import-export business?’

Anna stared at him. ‘You’re joking, of course.’

‘No, I’m not, and I was wondering if you’d put in a word for me. The idea of travelling about appeals to me very much and I’m acquainted with most of Europe. As you know Mother and I travelled abroad both summer and winter until a short while ago, and I get on well with people. Your boss must be in need of up and coming young men so what about it, Anna?’

‘I’m not sure,’ answered Anna doubtfully. ‘I’ve only worked for him such a short time myself that I'm reluctant to ask any favours.'

'But you will?' His voice was coaxing, and she felt herself beginning to weaken. 'Please, darling. It means so much to me.'

She couldn't resist him any longer. 'Yes, I'll ask Mr. Chatham if there's an opening, but don't pin your hopes on his offering you a job. He strikes me as very uncompromising, and if he doesn't want you I'm sure he'll say so right away.'

'Then your conscience needn't trouble you,' said Ricky cheerfully, 'because obviously he won't be conned into anything.'

'No, that's true,' agreed Anna, feeling a little better about it. 'I don't know exactly when he'll be back in England, Ricky, so you might have to wait a few weeks.'

'I thought you mentioned he might return in a fortnight.'

'He did say so but I haven't heard anything since he left and Mrs. Mabledon says that sometimes he stays in London and doesn't come down here.'

'Then we'll have to hope for the best. I shouldn't think he'd delay his next visit too long because he's bound to want to see what kind of a job you're making of running the house.'

Anna thought that too, and as the days went by she found herself tensing every time the telephone rang. When Drewe Chatham did return at last he took her completely by surprise, and she was far from being as cool and poised as she'd intended. She was so sure he would arrive at the weekend that she allowed herself to relax during the week, and she and Jeremy had been cleaning the car so that they were both hot and grubby. She was wearing a pair of faded jeans and an old shirt, and Jeremy had nothing on but a pair of bathing trunks because they intended swimming in the pool as soon as they'd finished.

When they heard the sound of a car Anna put her hand to her mouth in horror. 'Heavens, don't say it's visitors. I can't possibly face anyone looking like this.'

'Whoever it is is driving right round to the garage,' said Jeremy. 'It must be Drewe. Yes, it is.'

The long black car slid to a halt outside the garage, and Drewe Chatham got out. In spite of the hot weather he was dressed conservatively in a dark suit, and she felt acutely conscious of the shabbiness of her clothes and her tousled hair.

He raised his eyebrows. 'You look very busy. No crises while I've been away?'

'None,' she answered formally. 'Everything's gone very well.'

'Good. I'll go and change into something cooler. I flew back from Brussels this morning, and I feel as if I'm in a straitjacket.'

He disappeared, and Anna said to Jeremy: 'I think we'll call it a day; we've practically finished anyway. Would you ask Mrs. Mabledon for a jug of lemonade and plenty of ice? I think your brother would probably appreciate a long, cold drink.'

'Shall I take it down to the pool?'

'That's a good idea. I'll just make myself look a bit more respectable.'

She rushed to her room to drag on lilac linen slacks and a matching top over her swimsuit, then ran down to the pool. Drewe Chatham was already there, swimming with a powerful crawl and then diving down to the bottom. Jeremy had brought out the lemonade in a tall, frosted jug, and presently his stepbrother emerged, striding dripping across the grass to pour himself a drink.

'That's good,' he said. 'No one makes lemonade like Mrs. M.'

'I wondered afterwards if you'd have preferred something stronger,' said Anna.

'Not at this time of the day.'

His legs were brown and muscular, and Anna couldn't help noticing his narrow waist and broad shoulders. He hadn't acquired that tan on the pavements of Brussels, but she was quite ready to believe that he had plenty of invitations to go further afield at the weekends.

To distract her thoughts she said hurriedly: 'I'm afraid we weren't expecting you otherwise Sara would have stayed in. She's gone into Occambridge to collect some things from the cleaners.'

'I see,' he said non-committally. 'And how have you been getting on, Jeremy?'

'Fine,' answered Jeremy warily. 'Anna's been coaching me in tennis. She's got a jolly strong service for a woman.'

'Has she? There seems to be no end to her talents,' said Drewe Chatham smoothly, and Anna felt her colour rise. Fortunately Jeremy rescued her from further embarrassment by saying: 'Race you across the pool, Anna. You promised you would when we'd finished the car.'

'So I did.'

Thankful to be out of the range of her employer's speculative gaze Anna slipped out of her slacks and shirt and dived into the water, Jeremy following. She held herself back so that she wasn't too far ahead when she reached the other side, and he gasped: 'I'm doing better than I did at first, aren't I? It won't be long before I can beat you.'

'No, it won't,' she agreed, and then a voice behind them said: 'It could even be these holidays with a little more coaching,' and treading water she turned her head to see Drewe Chatham at her elbow.

'Do you think I could ever do the crawl?' asked Jeremy eagerly, and Drewe answered: 'Certainly you could. Want to try now?' and began a course of instruction there and then.

Anna swam away and left them to it. She was very fond of Jeremy, but he needed a man to give him confidence and his stepbrother could do a lot for him. She wondered how long Drewe Chatham was staying this time and whether he was satisfied with the way she was running the house. At least he hadn't criticised anything so far.

Sara arrived home in time for a swim before dinner, and didn't seem overjoyed to learn of her stepbrother's presence. It was as if she went out of her way to provoke him because she came into the dining-room in bare feet with a crumpled see-through shirt unbuttoned over her bikini.

Drewe surveyed her in disgust.

'You're not sitting down to dinner dressed, or rather undressed, like that. Go upstairs and put some clothes on.'

He was quite justified, Anna acknowledged, but she wished he could have been a trifle more tactful because Sara reacted furiously.

'You can't order me about like a child!'

'I can when you behave like one,' he retorted, unmoved. 'Now hurry up or you'll get no dinner.'

With her teeth set Sara rushed out of the room and Anna fully expected that she wouldn't return, but Sara was hungry and she knew that Drewe was quite capable of making certain that Mrs. Mabledon didn't hold back any of the stuffed veal or strawberry mousse for her. She came back wearing jeans with a clean shirt, and the rest of the meal passed off uneventfully.

When it was over Sara disappeared immediately to her room while Anna and Jeremy embarked on a game of draughts before he went to bed. Usually after that she read or watched television in the drawing-room, but tonight her employer was in there and she didn't know quite what to do. She hesitated in the hall after going up to say good night to Jeremy, and was about to walk out into the garden when Drewe Chatham appeared.

'Come and have a drink,' he said. 'I want to talk to you.'

She followed him into the drawing-room and said: 'Do you wish to see my accounts? I've kept a record of everything I've spent.'

'I haven't the slightest desire to see your accounts. Sit down and relax.

Sherry or gin and something?'

'I don't want a drink, thank you,' said Anna, but she sat down obediently in the corner of the sofa.

'Well, I do.' Drewe Chatham poured himself a whisky and seated himself opposite to her. 'I've had one hell of a week and I'm not in the mood for wrestling with Sara but her future needs to be settled. At present she's frittering her days away.'

'I think that like many young people she hasn't any real idea what she wants to do.'

His eyes glinted sardonically. 'You're Methuselah, I take it?'

'No, and I didn't mean to imply that I was a lot wiser at her age but there wasn't so much uncertainty then. She'll grow out of this phase, I'm sure.'

'She'd better, and in the meantime she needs something definite to occupy her even if it doesn't lead to any particular qualification.'

'She definitely isn't intellectual so I think any kind of academic course is ruled out. There isn't anything very suitable in Occambridge unless she attends classes in shorthand and typing at the Technical College, but she did show some interest in a modelling course so I wondered if you'd like me to make enquiries about one.'

'Yes, if that's what she wants. Anything's preferable to idleness.'

'It's difficult for her,' pointed out Anna. 'She was looking forward to a mild social whirl after leaving school, and she feels resentful about what's happened.'

'I know, but life deals us these blows and she'll have to learn to adjust. If she doesn't conquer her bitterness it will warp her, and that would be a pity.'

He spoke quite gently, and suddenly Anna's sympathy rose for him. After all, he'd lost his father too, and it couldn't have been easy for him to find himself responsible for a stepbrother and sister. It had affected his life as well as theirs, and altered his plans considerably.

'Jeremy seems to be settling down

better,' remarked Anna.

'Yes, I thought he looked much more relaxed than the last time I saw him. And you — how are you liking the life here?'

'I enjoy it. Mrs. Mabledon runs the house so competently that I'm scarcely earning my salary.'

He didn't say: 'Nonsense, you're doing a very good job,' or anything like that but instead gave a huge yawn, and for the first time Anna noticed the lines of fatigue under his tan.

'You look as if you could do with an early night,' she said.

'Yes, I haven't had much sleep lately,' and without more ado he rose to his feet, said over his shoulder : 'Good night, Miss Blakeney,' and was gone. Anna thought he was the most unpredictable man she'd ever met and settled down to watch a television programme, hoping fervently that Sara would have the sense not to annoy her stepbrother any further while he was down at Heathlands.

Drewe Chatham went up to London after breakfast the next morning, and didn't return until dinner. Anna dropped a hint that he'd seemed to look quite favourably on the idea of a modelling course, but Sara was still brooding over the previous night's episode and didn't respond. However, she appeared respectably attired that evening which passed off without incident.

It was at breakfast the following morning that Drewe said to Sara: 'I've managed to get tickets for a show in town tonight. We can have an early meal before we set off.'

Her eyes sparkled. 'Tickets for the Boysenberries show?' This was a new West End musical featuring the latest pop group, and playing to packed houses.

Drewe raised his eyebrows. 'Heavens, no, for 'The Man Beyond the Pale'.'

'Oh, that.' Sara shrugged. 'Oh well, I suppose it's better than nothing.'

'Don't overdo the gratitude,' said

Drewe sarcastically.

Anna never thought of asking Sara what she intended to wear and acknowledged afterwards that it would probably have made no difference if she had, but she was appalled when the girl entered the dining-room wearing denims and a cheesecloth smock and carrying a long, gaudily striped coat trimmed with monkey fur.

Her stepbrother took one look at her, then said decisively: 'I've no intention of taking you a yard in that outfit. Take it off immediately, and put on some decent clothes.'

Sara's chin jutted out obstinately. 'I will not. If you weren't unbelievably stuffy you'd realise that my generation doesn't go in for dressing up. Just because Althea looks like a dog's dinner every time you take her out it doesn't mean that I have to follow suit.'

'We'll leave Althea out of this,' said Drewe with dangerous calm. 'I'll give you ten minutes to change, otherwise you stay at home.'

'That won't worry me.' Sara sat down, looking ostentatiously indifferent.

'Right.' Drewe wasted no more time in argument but turned to Anna. 'It seems a pity to waste the ticket, however. Would you care to go to the theatre, Miss Blakeney?'

3

Anna was so surprised that she gaped at him, then because it was a play she very much wanted to see she couldn't resist saying: 'Yes, I would.'

She was aware that Sara was looking at her scornfully and reflected ruefully that this wasn't going to make the relationship between them any easier, but decided that the girl had only herself to blame for what had happened.

'Can you be ready in a quarter of an hour?' asked Drewe Chatham as they rose from dinner, and she answered: 'Yes.'

She managed it too, sliding into her black moiré suit with its frothy white blouse in record time. She still felt breathless as they drove away and wondered what they would find to talk about, but this proved to be no problem since her employer didn't appear to be in a conversational mood and concentrated on driving.

When they reached the city he said: 'Since it's a fine night I imagine you won't object to walking a little way so that I can park in a mews where some friends of mine live. As they're out of England at the moment I know they'll have no objection to my occupying their frontage.'

He turned into the mews, and the car came to rest outside a gay yellow front door flanked by two bay trees.

'I've always wanted to live in a place like this,' remarked Anna. 'You're in the city, yet apart from it.'

'It's a very compact house,' said her employer. 'Ideal for a couple, but hopeless where there are children.'

'Of course. You have a flat in Belgravia, haven't you, Mr. Chatham?'

'Yes, a service flat. Hardly big enough to turn round in, but all I need is a place to eat and sleep.'

'For the moment,' said Anna.

He looked at her interrogatively.

'You told me you would be getting married soon,' she explained, 'so I imagined you were probably looking out for something larger.'

'Yes,' he agreed uncommunicatively, and Anna took it as a hint to change the subject.

The play lived up to the praises of the critics in the Sunday papers, and Anna thoroughly enjoyed it. It seemed so long since she'd been taken out for the evening that her pleasure was intensified, and perhaps some of it was communicated to her companion because he exerted himself to entertain her and she found herself responding.

When they came out of the theatre he said: 'You didn't manage to eat much at dinner so we'll find a place for supper.'

'Won't that make us very late arriving home? I should be quite happy with a sandwich.'

'Nonsense, you need more than that. There's a little restaurant not far from here which is quite good.'

They turned a corner only to encounter a car coming towards them at a reckless speed. It swerved violently, and as it did so Drewe Chatham gave Anna a push which sent her reeling against the wall. The next instant the car had mounted the pavement and dealt him a glancing blow which flung him to the ground before roaring off without stopping. The whole incident was over in a flash, and as Anna recovered her balance and rushed forward Drewe Chatham was already picking himself up.

'Are you all right?' she gasped anxiously. 'If it hadn't been for you I should have been badly injured. You saved my life.'

'Don't fuss,' he said. 'Let's get away from here.'

He was cupping his right elbow with his left hand and Anna saw that he was very white round the mouth.

'You're hurt,' she said. 'You need an ambulance and we ought to contact the police.'

'That's the last thing I intend to do. It was a hit and run driver, probably drunk, and since I didn't get his number what hope have the police of tracing him? We'll walk to the mews and you can drive me home.'

'But you're not fit to walk anywhere,' protested Anna.

'Why must women always argue? The sooner we reach home the sooner I'll be comfortable.'

He began to walk, and Anna had no option but to accompany him. By the time they reached the mews she could see beads of sweat on his brow, and she made one more attempt to persuade him to seek some treatment.

'At least see a doctor before we start back for Heathlands,' she urged, but he ignored this and countered with: 'Do you think you can drive this car?'

'Of course,' she snapped, nettled at his obvious doubts as to her competence, and sliding behind the wheel turned as skilfully as she could out of the mews. She was relieved to find that the car handled beautifully, and since once she was out of the city there wasn't much traffic on the roads she was able to make good time. All the same, it was a nightmare journey. Drewe Chatham was grey under his tan, and from the way he was holding his arm Anna was pretty sure his collar bone was broken. She was haunted by the fear that he would collapse before they reached Heathlands, and breathed a great sigh of relief when the house came into sight.

She helped him out of the car and into the house where he sank into the nearest chair, closing his eyes. Anna called Mrs. Mabledon to fetch the brandy, then telephoned the doctor who arrived in a very short time, and confirmed that Drewe Chatham had broken his collar bone. Jeremy, aroused by the commotion, had come downstairs and Anna tried to persuade him to return to bed.

'I'll bring you some warm milk to help you to sleep,' she promised.

‘Is Drewe badly hurt?’ he asked fearfully.

‘No,’ she assured him. ‘He’s broken his collar bone, but in a few weeks he’ll be back to normal again.’

‘It’s a judgement on him for refusing to take me to the theatre,’ declared Sara, and Anna sighed.

‘How can you be so silly? It’s the kind of thing which could happen to anyone. As a matter of fact, I would have been the victim if your stepbrother hadn’t pushed me to one side.’

Jeremy squeezed her arm. ‘I’m sorry Drewe has been hurt, but I’m glad it wasn’t you.’

Sara said nothing more but disappeared upstairs while the doctor helped his patient to bed. When he came down again he said to Anna: ‘I’ve given him a sedative so he should sleep now, but I want him to have an X-ray tomorrow to make sure there are no complications. Can you drive him to the hospital about half past ten?’

‘Yes, of course,’ said Anna, and when

the doctor had left Mrs. Mabledon brought in a bowl of soup on a tray.

'I thought you might like this as you missed your supper. Things could have turned out very much worse, but all the same Mr. Drewe isn't going to take kindly to having his activities curtailed.'

'I don't suppose he is,' agreed Anna, and suddenly realised that her employer would probably be part of the household for the next few weeks, a prospect which filled her with dismay.

She duly drove him to the hospital next morning, and later drove him back with his plastered arm in a sling. She had expected him to be extremely irritable and curse his ill-luck, but he said very little at all. Then as they arrived back at Heathlands she ventured: 'Does this mean you'll be down here for a while? You won't stay in the London flat by yourself, will you?'

'I don't see why not.'

'Surely it would be very depressing and not at all comfortable.'

'Why this eagerness to have me down here?'

'I'm not eager to have you down here — no, I don't mean that, it's just that I think it would be better for you and better for Jeremy.'

'Ah, now I understand. It's Jeremy's welfare you're concerned about.'

'Naturally since I'm employed to look after him,' retorted Anna, 'and I think it would be good for him to have a man about the house.'

'Then my accident hasn't been entirely a disaster.'

Anna drew a breath of sheer exasperation. Her employer seemed to take a delight in twisting everything she said and making her feel a fool.

'All right,' he said unexpectedly, 'I know what you've been trying to say, and I'm happy to tell you that I've decided to remain here for a week at least. It will be far pleasanter at Heathlands than in London, and while I'm here I'll make an effort to get to know Jeremy better. I've never really had much to do with him, and since I'm his guardian now I must remedy that.'

'And Sara?'

'Sara's a different proposition. The sooner she's fixed up with a definite occupation the better.'

'I'll start making enquiries about modelling courses tomorrow.'

Drewe Chatham's accident had temporarily banished Ricky from Anna's mind, and it wasn't until she answered the telephone the following morning and heard his voice that she remembered her promise to mention him to her employer.

'Hello, Anna,' he said. 'Will it be all right if I come down on Sunday as usual?'

She hesitated. 'Ricky, I don't know. Mr. Chatham's here. He's had an accident and broken his collar bone so he's likely to remain at Heathlands for a while.'

'Oh, I see. You don't think he'd approve of my visiting you?'

'Well . . . ' Anna suddenly became conscious that Sara was at her elbow.

'Is that Ricky you're speaking to?' the girl demanded. 'Let me have a word with him,' and she snatched the receiver out of Anna's hand.

'Ricky, you must come down this weekend,' she cried. 'I want you to and there isn't the slightest reason why you shouldn't,' and she dropped the receiver, saying to Anna: 'I've finished now.'

'Sara seems to think I'll be welcome,' Ricky remarked, and Anna answered helplessly: 'Then you'd better come.'

'Have you had an opportunity to sound Mr. Chatham out about me?'

'Not yet, but I'll make one before Sunday. Don't be too hopeful, Ricky. There may not be an opening at the moment.'

Anna didn't find it easy to approach her employer the next day on Ricky's behalf, but she forced herself to say: 'There was something I wanted to ask you, Mr. Chatham.'

'Yes?' He looked up from the magazine he was leafing through.

'I wondered if there were any vacancies in your office. A friend of mine is working in London for a firm of interior decorators, but he isn't very happy with the job which he only regards as a stop-gap.'

'A boy-friend?'

'Well, yes,' admitted Anna.

'What did he do previously?'

'He ran an antique shop but that was to please his mother who clung to him and begged him not to leave home. Now she's dead, and he wants to embark on a worthwhile career.'

'I see. Well, we've always room for someone with enthusiasm, but I shan't be able to see him until I go back to town.'

'As a matter of fact, he'll be coming down here on Sunday. When he arrived in London he called to see me, and Sara invited him to drop in at weekends to swim in the pool. I hope you don't mind.'

Her employer looked at her keenly. 'No, I don't mind. I'll have a word with him on Sunday.'

Ricky arrived after lunch as usual, and Anna went to meet him with a lift of her heart. Not that she had much opportunity for a word alone with him. There was only time to murmur: 'I've broken the ice for you,' when Sara was urging him out to the pool with: 'Come on, Ricky, don't let's waste a second of this heavenly weather.'

Drewe Chatham was stretched out in a long chair, wearing sailcloth slacks and a blue shirt, his fair hair glinting in the sun. Sara forestalled Anna by performing an introduction, and then Ricky went to change into his swimming trunks. Anna saw her employer studying him, and wondered how Ricky was measuring up to that cool appraisal. She was glad to see that it didn't appear to affect him and that he was his natural self, chaffing Sara and patiently showing Jeremy how to dive.

They had tea in the garden, and when they'd finished Drewe said: 'Jeremy, push the trolley inside, will you? Sara, could you look for that book I was talking about a little while ago?'

'Oh, there's no hurry,' responded Sara airily. 'I'll find it before Ricky leaves.'

'Find it now, please,' said Drewe firmly, and with a bad grace Sara walked towards the house together with Anna and Jeremy.

'Who does Drewe think he is?' she fumed. 'If he imagines I'm going to bow down to him he's very much mistaken. He may be my guardian but I shall be eighteen in three weeks and then I shall be free to do as I like.'

'Hardly, until you're earning your own living,' pointed out Anna.

'Oh, I'm aware Drewe controls the money Daddy left in trust for Jeremy and me until we're twenty-one, but even so he isn't going to dictate to me.'

'I don't imagine he wants to do that,' said Anna mildly.

'Don't delude yourself. He's suffering from a power complex but I'm not one of the minions in his office, ready to crawl to him.'

Hoping that his manoeuvre meant that her employer wanted a word alone with Ricky, Anna managed to keep the others inside the house for a quarter of an hour, and by the time they went back to the pool Ricky's grin told her that he was feeling pleased with life. He stayed on to dinner, and before he left he was able to tell her that he'd been offered a job.

'It means beginning at the bottom, naturally, but there are good prospects.'

'When do you start?'

'Officially I'm supposed to give Hilary a month's notice, but I'm pretty sure she'll release me in a week. Bless you, Anna, for your help.'

He dropped a kiss on the tip of her nose, and then they sprang apart as Sara appeared.

'Oh, there you are, Ricky. Do you really have to leave so early? Can't you buy a car so that you'd have your own transport?'

'Well now that I'm going to work for Chatham Exports I expect to be a millionaire pretty soon so I'll be looking out for a Rolls,' teased Ricky.

'So that was why Drewe wanted to get rid of me this afternoon, so that he could talk to you,' said Sara furiously, 'and Anna knew it. Why didn't you tell me what was going on, Ricky? I could have been just as much help to you as she was.'

She turned away in a huff but Ricky sprang after her, and Anna saw him put his arm round her shoulders as he exerted all his charm to soothe her. Anna herself was filled with a bubbling happiness. This was the chance Ricky had been waiting for, the chance which could make all the difference to his future and hers.

If she'd expected Drewe Chatham to comment on Ricky then she was to be disappointed since he made no reference to the visitor. To Anna's surprise

Sara announced the next day that she was tired of lazing about at home and wanted to start a modelling course forthwith. Anna had already made enquiries in that direction with the result that by the following week Sara had been enrolled on a six-months' course and was to travel up to London each day.

This made life a lot easier for Anna. With Sara occupied she was able to devote herself to Jeremy, and because she thought it was good for him to be with boys of his own age she encouraged him to invite friends to the house and took them for picnics and long walks in the country.

Drewe Chatham took things easy for a week and Anna grew used to sharing the drawing-room with him after dinner, discovering that he had a great love of classical music and enjoyed reading history and biography. Sara, no lover of Chopin, disappeared so Anna and her employer were alone together when Jeremy was in bed. She hadn't forgotten the imminence of Sara's birthday and took an early opportunity of mentioning it.

'I wondered if you were considering having any kind of celebration,' she said.

Drewe Chatham frowned. 'I hadn't really thought about it. Of course I imagine her parents would have given her a party, but under the circumstances . . . '

'It seems a pity not to mark the occasion in some way,' urged Anna. 'You could arrange dinner at a restaurant followed by a show or invite a few guests down here; whichever Sara would prefer.'

'Very well, I'll put it to her.'

Rather to Anna's surprise Sara opted for a small party at home, and drew up a list of a dozen people she wanted to invite. They included the two Frensham girls and their brother, a number of people she'd met in London, and Ricky. They all accepted so Anna held a consultation with Mrs. Mabledon.

'I think a buffet supper would be best, don't you?' suggested Anna, and Mrs. Mabledon agreed, adding: 'But I've no talent for creating appetising bits and pieces. Good, plain cooking's more my line.'

'That's all right, I know a woman who caters for buffet affairs and delivers everything on the day of the party. She was staying at the hotel in Cornwall where I worked, and she gave me her address in case I should ever need her services so I rang her up to see if she were still in business before I approached Mr. Chatham. She'll make all the fiddly things, and you can concentrate on your superb chocolate gateaux.'

'I'll be happy to do that.'

Anna went to infinite trouble to make the party a success in order to make up a little to Sara for the loss of her parents. Drewe Chatham had given her a generous sum to defray expenses so she decided to make it an outdoor party if the weather were fine and hired barbecue equipment, arranging to have fairy lights threaded through the trees in the garden and a spotlight trained on the pool. If it rained the barbecue would have to be transferred to the garage, but the guests probably wouldn't mind that.

Fortunately the day of the party was fine and quite warm. The buffet food was duly delivered after lunch, and Anna set it out in the dining-room on two trestle tables which she'd decorated in white and silver. Jeremy's eyes widened as he saw it.

'I don't have to go to bed early, do I?' he pleaded. 'I can stay up for the party, can't I?'

'Of course you can't,' said Sara, 'and anyway you'd be bored.'

'I wouldn't!' denied Jeremy vehemently.

'I thought perhaps he could hand round drinks when the guests first arrive, Sara, just to give him a glimpse of the party, and then go to bed,' suggested Anna tactfully.

'Well, no more than that and he's to go to bed without any fuss,' decreed Sara.

'But I want to join in the barbecue, and you're a beast, Sara, not to let me.'

'Look,' said Anna, taking him on one side, 'I'll make a bargain with you. It is Sara's birthday so I think she ought to have the kind of party she wants while at the same time you'd find it difficult to get near the barbecue for the other guests. Suppose tomorrow you have your own barbecue in the garden? You can invite three boys and do the cooking yourselves. It will be much more fun for you.'

'Can we cook whatever we like?'

'Within reason, yes, and if you go to bed without a fuss tonight I'll bring you a tray in bed with something of everything on it.'

Jeremy considered, and then said: 'All right. I'll ask Tom and Alastair and Graham to come tomorrow, and we'll have a super time.'

It was only at the last minute Anna

had time to change her dress. She'd meant to buy something new, but she hadn't had the opportunity to go up to London and there wasn't a good dress shop in Occambridge. She had to fall back on a printed banlon dress which she'd bought last year, but the inky blue background patterned with dull green, white and shocking pink suited her and she'd managed to have her hair set in a swirling style which gave her head the appearance of a flower on a slender stalk. Sara was in a floating yellow chiffon dress patterned with marguerites which made her look fragile and very young, and she put her head round Anna's door, saying: 'Aren't you ready yet? I can hear a car now.'

'I'm coming,' said Anna, and then as she passed Drewe's door he called: 'Can you give me a hand? It's not quite so easy to get into a coat as into a sweater.'

'I ought to have realised you might need some help,' said Anna, and having gently eased his arm into the coat sleeve she adjusted the sling.

'It's a confounded nuisance,' he said impatiently. 'I'll be glad when I can dispense with all these trappings. There's the bell so the first guest must be on the doorstep.'

It was Ricky, and to Anna's surprise he was driving a car.

'I couldn't manage any longer without my own transport,' he explained. 'She's by no means new but she packs a fair turn of speed.'

'There's no need for you to go back to town tonight,' said Sara. 'You can get up early tomorrow and I'll drive back with you. I've a class at ten in the morning.'

'Well . . . ' said Ricky. 'If you're sure there's a spare bed.'

'Of course there is,' declared Anna, and in her anxiety not to let Sara down she sounded more eager than she meant to. Drewe Chatham glanced at her but said nothing, and then another ring at the bell diverted their attention to the rest of the guests who arrived one after the other.

The evening went with a swing. The barbecue was very popular, and Drewe Chatham managed to grill sausages and cutlets successfully in spite of having only one useful arm. Jeremy handed round drinks, and then went off to bed without demur. Anna, running up later with the promised plateful of food, found him sitting up in bed eagerly awaiting her arrival.

'I've brought you a taste of everything except chocolate gateau,' she said, 'and I'm saving that for you for tomorrow. I thought it might be too rich tonight on top of everything else.'

'Goody, smoked salmon,' said Jeremy. 'You won't let them grill all the sausages tonight, will you? You'll save some for us for tomorrow?'

'I put them on one side specially. Don't forget to clean your teeth before you go to sleep.'

Anna went downstairs again and into the kitchen where Mrs. Mabledon was packing dirty dishes into the dishwasher. 'I might as well get these done in relays,' she said. 'Well, they seem to be enjoying themselves though how they can stand that music I can't imagine.'

'Doesn't it set your blood tingling?' commented Anna, feeling the beat vibrate through her.

'It sets my teeth on edge but you're young,' shrugged Mrs. Mabledon tolerantly.

'That reminds me, Sara's invited Mr. Beeston to stay the night. The bed in the spare room is aired, isn't it?'

'Oh, it's aired,' agreed Mrs. Mabledon in a rather curious tone. 'I'll go and make it up. Is he staying just the one night?'

'Yes, he has to be at work in the morning. He's giving Sara a lift to London.'

'I see.' Mrs. Mabledon went off upstairs and Anna returned to the party.

Most of the guests were dancing to

the record player, and the long french windows of the drawing-room were open to the terrace. There was the sound of voices and laughter down by the pool, and Anna hoped that no one would fall in. She walked across the grass and saw the two Frensham girls and a couple of youths running round the rim of the pool, then to her relief they veered away from it towards the house.

From here the music was muted and she lingered a little, enjoying the night scents of the garden and the cool air. All at once she heard a sound and realised that it came from the changing cabin. Obviously there was someone inside, and after a moment's hesitation she walked up to it and called: 'Is anyone there?'

The cabin was divided into two cubicles, and after a swift movement in the right hand one Sara appeared.

'Yes, I'm here,' she answered impudently. 'Why, did you want me?'

'Not particularly,' said Anna, 'but I

heard a noise and thought I'd better investigate.'

'It was so hot that I came out here to cool off.'

It was the feeblest of excuses, and only underlined the fact that the girl wasn't alone in the cabin. Her attitude dared Anna to venture any further comment, and realising that she could do nothing Anna turned and went back to the house. She'd no intention of making a scene, but determined that if Sara weren't back in circulation in a quarter of an hour she would return to the cabin and refuse this time to be fobbed off.

But fortunately that wasn't necessary. Sara suddenly appeared again, dancing with the Frensham boy, and Anna wondered if he'd been her companion in the cabin. She was beginning to feel rather tired since she'd been up early that morning and had worked hard all day, but Sara and her contemporaries looked ready to continue dancing all night. Drewe

Chatham suddenly materialised and enquired: 'How's it going?'

'Very well, I think, judging by the way they seem to be enjoying themselves.'

He glanced at her sharply. 'You look tired.'

'Oh, I'm fine,' lied Anna.

'Really? Come into the kitchen.'

Puzzled, she followed him along the hall and into the kitchen where Mrs. Mabledon was stirring a large pot.

'I thought I'd give them some of my onion soup before they went home,' she said. 'I'll take it into the dining-room shortly, and that will give them a hint that the party's nearly over.'

'In the meantime we'll have a reviver,' said Drewe Chatham, and popped the cork of a bottle of champagne. Its delicious sparkle lifted Anna's spirits and dimmed her fatigue.

'I really shouldn't, Mr. Drewe,' protested Mrs. Mabledon, 'but I will this once. Good health.'

They finished the bottle in a companionable silence, and then Drewe said: 'I think we ought to serve that soup now since it will take a while for them to drink it.'

'Right,' said Mrs. Mabledon, and Anna helped her to pour it into a tureen and carry it into the dining-room. There was a basket of hot rolls with it, and the guests fell on both with cries of delight in spite of the fact that they'd been eating all evening.

At last they'd all gone except Ricky. His room was ready so Anna showed him to it and hoped he'd have a good night.

'I haven't enjoyed an evening so much for years,' he told her, 'but I don't imagine you had much fun.'

'I didn't expect to. It was Sara's party, and as long as she enjoyed it that's all that matters.'

He said: 'Sara's not a child, you know.'

'Not now she isn't. She's come of age.'

'I don't mean that. Anna — '

She looked at him. 'What is it?'

'Never mind, this isn't the time or the place. Good night.'

'Good night, Ricky,' and Anna went to her room feeling vaguely troubled for no good reason. She told herself that because she was tired she was imagining that Ricky was also uneasy. Why should he be when he'd just mentioned how much he'd enjoyed himself? Before he left the next morning she would manage a word with him and suggest that they had an evening out together. Now that he had a car they wouldn't be dependent on the train service to town, and could do a theatre without having to consider the time.

But there wasn't any opportunity to get him alone. Both Sara and Ricky were hard to rouse in the morning, and they'd only time to bolt a cup of coffee and a piece of toast before leaving. Ricky thanked her in one brief sentence, and Anna could only hope that the traffic wouldn't be so heavy as to delay them at all. Then a car called for

Drewe Chatham who was now travelling to his office each day, and she was left to organise affairs for herself and Jeremy.

He was full of excitement at the prospect of having his own party. Anna didn't feel in the least like coping with four small boys, but she'd promised and she wouldn't go back on her word. She telephoned the mothers of Tom, Alastair and Graham and arranged to pick the boys up after lunch, then she persuaded Jeremy to draw up a programme of events, a task which occupied him for the rest of the morning.

Fortunately the weather was kind again so the party started off with a swim for everyone, then the barbecue which had been lit earlier on was pronounced ready to grill the sausages. There were plenty of these since Anna was aware that the boys wouldn't have the patience to wait while chops or steaks were cooked properly, and there were more of the hot rolls which Mrs.

Mabledon had provided the previous evening together with crisps, savoury sticks, cheese dips and the chocolate gateau which Jeremy loved. It was a fearsome mixture, but the boys washed it down with unlimited Coca-Cola and appeared to be enjoying themselves tremendously.

When they couldn't eat any more they played a game of cricket with special rules which Tom invented. A hit into the pool counted as a boundary with the result that they spent nearly all their time jumping into the water to retrieve the ball, and they were making so much noise that they never heard the sound of a car until Anna, leaping into the air for a catch off Alastair, found herself almost in the arms of Drewe Chatham who had come up behind her.

'Oh,' she said in confusion. 'I didn't know you were back.'

'So I realise. What on earth are you doing? I thought you'd be resting after last night's hectic proceedings.'

'This is Jeremy's party. I promised

him one when he went to bed so co-operatively last night.'

'You're a glutton for punishment, aren't you?'

'Come and help field, Drewe,' begged Jeremy.

'Oh no,' said Anna quickly. 'You might damage your arm.'

'I'll risk it,' he said, and batting one-handed managed to knock up a better score than anyone else.

When the guests had gone and Jeremy had announced that he didn't think he wanted very much dinner Anna was able to relax. She was tired but happy, and with dinner over and Jeremy in bed she sat in the drawing-room listening to a violin concerto on the hi-fi and trying not to fall asleep.

'I have to congratulate you,' remarked her employer suddenly. 'You made a good job of yesterday's party.'

'It's quite easy to organise things when you're given the money to do it, and you were very generous.'

'Nevertheless you worked hard, and

then there was this affair today.'

'That was nothing really; just a frolic for Jeremy. I wanted him to have a last treat before he goes back to school.'

'Good Lord, I'd forgotten that was in the offing. When does he go?'

'The day after tomorrow.'

'Has he got everything he needs?'

'I think so. I've been through the Matron's list and bought one or two things on your account.'

'Good. By the way, I'm afraid you'll have to take him back. I shall be going along to the hospital to have this plaster off, and then staying in London for the next few days.'

'I see.' Anna hesitated, and then went on: 'I was wondering since Jeremy's going back to school whether you'll need me here any longer.'

'You'd better stay on for the time being,' decided Drewe Chatham crisply. 'I shall be going abroad again very soon so I want someone in charge here. I'll let you know when you're redundant.'

Anna felt chilled. A moment ago he'd

been praising her, but now it was as if he'd repented of this laxity and had returned to treating her in his usual impersonal manner.

She said: 'I think I'll go to bed. I'm more tired than I realised. Good night.'

Alone in her room she shivered a little, though not from cold. Jeremy was the only one in the house who showed any warmth in his relationship towards her, and in two days he would be gone. Wouldn't it be wiser of her to take her departure now? After all, Jeremy would have to learn to do without her eventually. Then she knew she couldn't desert him, not until he was less vulnerable and able to stand up to life more easily.

Drewe Chatham went up to London as usual the next morning, and the following day Anna drove Jeremy to school. He was very subdued on the journey and his eyes were suspiciously bright when she said goodbye to him, but two of the milling horde of little boys rushed up to greet him and Anna guessed that he would soon settle down.

'You'll come and take me out when I have my exeat, won't you?' he begged. 'I'll write and tell you when it is. We usually have lunch at the Fairacre Arms.'

'Either I'll come or your stepbrother will,' promised Anna. 'Now I must go.'

'Come on, Chatty, there's sardines on toast for supper and a film afterwards,' said a red-headed tough, and Jeremy looking more cheerful Anna seized the opportunity to leave him.

All the way back to Heathlands she thought about him, almost as if she were his mother, and the house seemed silent and empty without him. Sara was out most evenings now, either staying on in London or meeting Isobel Frensham who was going up to university next month, so Anna found the time dragging. She occupied herself in the house as much as she could but there wasn't a lot for her to do, and Mrs. Mabledon, bringing her dinner in one evening, said: 'Why don't you take the opportunity while Jeremy's away to get around a bit? When he's home again you'll be tied to the house so make the most of your freedom. What about that young man of yours? Isn't he going to take you out at all?'

'I don't suppose he realises I'm free because I forgot to tell him that Jeremy had gone back to school. I'll ring him up tonight and have a word with him.'

She ate her meal then went straight to the telephone, but to her disappointment there was no reply from Ricky's flat. Of course it was more than likely he would be out so tomorrow she would ring his office and if he were busy leave a message for him to call her. However, she managed to get him on the line, but when she suggested their meeting he sounded curiously evasive and said: 'It's a bit difficult at the moment, Anna. I can't always get away when I want to.'

'You mean you're working a lot of overtime? Not every night, surely?'

'No, not as often as that. I'll fix something and give you a ring. What would you like to do, see a show or dance?'

'I don't really mind. It seems such a long time since we were able to talk freely together.'

'Yes, and I can't ask you here to the flat because I never know when the others will be in. I must go now, but I'll be in touch.'

He sounded anxious to get away, and Anna was conscious of uneasiness when she put down the receiver. Surely there was nothing wrong with his job? She hadn't seen much of Ricky since he started at Chatham Exports, but he'd seemed cheerful and confident at the party. She waited for him to ring and tried to push her worries to the back of her mind.

Two days after he'd dispensed with his sling Drewe Chatham flew to Brussels, but when the weekend passed and Anna still hadn't heard from Ricky she lowered her pride to ask Sara if she knew what he was doing.

Sara hesitated for a moment, then she said: 'Well, as a matter of fact he's not coming down here just at present because I prefer to meet him in London instead. This may come as a shock to you, but Ricky and I want to get married.'

4

'Married?' gasped Anna, sure that she couldn't have heard properly. 'You can't be serious. You've only known each other a few weeks.'

Sara tossed her head. 'Time has nothing to do with it. You can fall in love in a matter of minutes, and the first time I saw Ricky I knew he was the man for me.'

'But Ricky — ?'

'He feels the same way. Of course I realise he was your friend first but there was never any definite engagement between you, was there?'

'No,' agreed Anna numbly. 'We were never actually engaged.'

But I believed it was only a matter of time, she wanted to cry aloud. Oh, if only I'd never come here, if only I'd stayed in Cornwall then perhaps Ricky wouldn't have drifted to London and even if he had he wouldn't have met you. How could you do this to me, Ricky? Sara's hardly more than a child, you can't be in love with her!

She said unsteadily: 'You're so young, you'll meet other men. How can you be sure at eighteen that Ricky is the one for you?'

Sara gave her a sidelong glance. 'If you're trying to put me off him it won't work.'

'I'm not attempting that, only begging you to consider a little and not do anything in a hurry. Ricky hasn't spoken to your stepbrother, has he?'

'To Drewe? No, and there's no reason why he should. I don't have to ask Drewe's permission to get married.'

'No, not technically, but don't you think it would be a tactful thing to do?'

'I don't see why I should,' said Sara sulkily, but there was an edge of doubt in her voice. 'Do you mean that because Ricky's working for Chatham Exports we ought to play up to Drewe?'

'Not exactly, but it couldn't do any

harm to avoid issuing an ultimatum. Leave things until he's back in England and you can talk to him properly.'

'I suppose we could,' said Sara undecidedly. 'We didn't really mean to tell anyone yet, but I thought you ought to know.'

'Did Ricky ask you to break it to me?'

Sara looked slightly uncomfortable. 'No, as I said we'd agreed to keep our plans secret for the moment, but when you mentioned Ricky coming down here I thought you might have guessed something and it would be better to tell you.'

You wanted me to know because you're not absolutely sure that Ricky feels the same way about you as you do about him, hazarded Anna, and this is your way of forcing his hand. You're pretty, attractive and young so it isn't surprising that Ricky's flattered by the play you've made for him, but if he had time to consider he might come to his senses and so might you. At all costs I must persuade you not to do anything precipitate.

Aloud she said: 'Ricky really isn't earning enough to support a wife yet but it won't be long before he is. It won't do any harm to wait a little while before you break the news to your stepbrother, and by then Ricky will be more securely settled in the firm.'

Sara nodded. 'You could be right.'

So a crisis was avoided and since the secret was out Ricky came down to Heathlands the next weekend. Seeing Sara's possessive attitude towards him Anna wondered how she could have been so blind the night of the party. Now it was quite obvious who had been concealed with her in the bathing cabin; it must have been Ricky all the time.

He didn't flaunt his relationship with Sara in front of Anna but he took care not to give her any opportunity of tackling him about it, in fact he kept out of her way as much as he could and was careful never to be alone with her. She had to preserve an appearance of normality but she was so sick at heart that she was on the point of asking Ricky point-blank what had gone wrong between them, if she'd been mistaken in thinking that he'd loved her, then realised that there was nothing to be gained by it. If he'd ever cared for her at all he didn't now, and the humiliation of discovering that Sara had brought him to the point of marriage in a few short weeks while her own relationship with him had drifted on for two years kept her from reproaching him. She would at least hold on to her dignity and self-respect though there was little comfort to be gained from that.

Certainly Anna had to summon all her resolution to conceal her unhappiness. She suspected that Mrs. Mabledon guessed at the situation, but the older woman said nothing and Anna was grateful to her for her restraint. There was a faint hope that gradually Sara's feeling for Ricky might lose some of its intensity, but that wasn't likely to happen before her stepbrother arrived home. Then all at once he rang through from Brussels to say that instead of coming back to England he would be flying out to India and would probably remain there for a couple of months.

'Nothing untoward has cropped up while I've been over here, has it?' he queried.

'No,' lied Anna.

For a moment she was tempted to tell him about Sara and Ricky but she knew she had no right to do that, also in two months the situation could alter completely. They might not even be speaking to each other by then.

But if she were prepared to be patient Sara wasn't.

'Two months!' she raged. 'Drewe's no right to call himself our guardian when he goes away like this. Anything might happen to me or to Jeremy while he's at the other side of the world.'

'Your stepbrother does provide for you,' pointed out Anna. 'It isn't as if you were left alone, and he could fly back to England in a few hours if anything went wrong.'

Sara flounced out but didn't allude to the matter again, and Anna imagined that she'd reconciled herself to waiting. In this she was quite wrong. Sara didn't take kindly to being thwarted, and having been indulged by her father and given a good deal of her own way she didn't see why she should have to postpone her plans now.

That she'd written to her stepbrother and told him she wanted to get married Anna had no idea so that it was a tremendous shock when a few days later as she was making out a shopping list preparatory to going into Occambridge the front door slammed and Drewe Chatham stalked into the room.

Anna gaped at him in astonishment, and then said: 'We didn't expect you home, Mr. Chatham. Is there anything wrong?'

'You don't imagine that I've postponed my trip to India and endured an abominably bumpy flight just for the fun of it, do you?' he enquired sarcastically. 'How far has this ridiculous affair of Sara's gone?'

Anna went very white, and his eyes narrowed.

'So you did know about it, and yet you let me believe that everything was as usual here.'

'I didn't feel that I'd any right to mention it at this stage,' stammered Anna, 'because Sara promised me that she'd wait until you came home to break the news to you.'

'Well, she didn't. She wrote and told me she intended to marry Beeston, forcing me to cancel a trip which I'd taken a great deal of trouble to arrange and probably losing me a considerable amount of money. It was because I didn't want to have to worry about this kind of thing going on behind my back that I paid you to look after the household.'

Now that she'd weathered the initial shock Anna's anger began to rise.

'Until recently I was as much in the dark as you were,' she said. 'Since Sara's away in London most of the week I can't possibly know of all the people she's meeting and even if I did I couldn't control her movements. She's no longer a child.'

'I'm aware of that, but she didn't meet this fellow in London, did she? You brought him down here.'

Anna's anger had already ebbed because she was too miserable to sustain it.

'That's true,' she admitted, 'but I'd no idea they would fall in love with each other.'

Drewe Chatham started to say something, then changed his mind and remarked in a milder tone: 'I don't suppose you had since in Sara's case I believe it's more the idea of being in love rather than the actual person which has influenced her. As for Beeston — ' Once again he stopped, then continued: 'At all events, the idea of her getting married yet is quite ridiculous and I shall forbid anything more than an engagement for a year. Now I'll have some coffee, collect a few papers and go up to my office. Tell Sara she's to stay in this evening.'

'Certainly,' answered Anna, and then went along to the kitchen to acquaint Mrs. Mabledon with what had happened.

'So Mr. Drewe's flown home, has he?' commented Mrs. Mabledon, 'and in a fine temper too, I'll be bound.'

'That sums it up,' admitted Anna.

'Sara's a foolish child to put his back up deliberately, but she's so headstrong that she must have her own way in everything. What does she think she's going to live on if she gets married with Mr. Beeston only just started in his job?' Mrs. Mabledon looked at Anna, and said deliberately : 'At first I thought that he came down to see you and that the pair of you would make a match of it.'

'We've been friends for a long time,' said Anna, trying to speak lightly, 'but we were never actually engaged. When he left Cornwall knowing that I was near London he naturally came to look me up. Now I wish he hadn't.'

'No,' agreed Mrs. Mabledon thoughtfully. 'Still, who knows what will happen in a year's time? If Sara keeps on with this modelling course she will meet all kinds of people and may change her mind about wanting to get married. If she does perhaps your friend won't be entirely broken-hearted. She's made no secret of the fact that she finds him attractive, and it would take a very level-headed man to resist such a pretty girl when she throws herself at his head.'

There was a lot of sense in what Mrs. Mabledon said, and Anna felt her hopes rise ever so slightly. If Ricky had been dazzled by Sara's looks a year would give him a chance to decide whether her temperament matched them, a breathing space before he committed himself entirely, and as the housekeeper hinted Sara might also change her mind.

Drewe Chatham drank his coffee,

then left for London, returning in the early evening. Sara was back before him, and tossed her head defiantly when Anna gave her his message.

'I'll stay in with pleasure,' she said. 'I intend to get it all settled.'

But her stepbrother wasn't to be forced into anything. When they met he said curtly: 'We'll postpone our discussion until after dinner, Sara. There's no point in arguing over the meal.'

'There's no need for any discussion either,' retorted Sara pertly. 'I'm of age and I shall marry Ricky with or without your permission.'

'We'll go into that later,' he answered, quite unmoved, and ate his dinner without addressing another remark to her. Because it was unbearable to sit there in stony silence Anna began to ask him questions about his proposed trip to India, and would have enjoyed hearing about a previous visit he'd paid to the country if the atmosphere hadn't been so strained. As it was she had to force her food down and in spite of her brave words Sara pushed her helping of chocolate pudding round and round her plate, obviously finding it difficult to swallow.

Her interview with her stepbrother lasted only a short time, but from her raised voice it was evidently a stormy one. Because she wanted to avoid overhearing anything even by accident Anna walked into the garden, but it was chilly out there and when she came in to pick up a coat it was to see Sara burst out of the study, her face flushed and furious, and storm up the stairs.

Anna went into the drawing-room, her face troubled. It was plain that Sara hadn't taken kindly to her stepbrother's ultimatum which meant that it wasn't going to be very comfortable in her vicinity for the next few days. Drewe Chatham didn't emerge from his study again that evening, and in the morning he announced that he was leaving for London immediately after breakfast and flying out to Brussels that afternoon.

'I've told Sara that there is to be no marriage for a year,' he informed Anna, 'and when I call in at my office today I shall have a few strong words to say to Beeston. He had no right to propose marriage to her until his finances were on a sound basis. How on earth does he think he can support a wife on what he's earning at present?'

Anna remained silent, not knowing what to say for the best. She had a feeling that her employer didn't care much for Ricky and wasn't surprised at this for no two men could have been more unlike. Ricky's charm was spontaneous. He had none of the cool calculation of the other man, and it was easy to see why Sara had fallen in love so rapidly.

She came home that evening prepared to argue afresh with her stepbrother and was annoyed to find him gone.

'If he thinks that I shall sit down meekly and allow him to dictate to me then he can think again,' she fumed.

Since it was no longer warm enough

to bathe in the pool Ricky had stopped coming down to Heathlands so that when Anna received a letter from the Knights who were occupying her cottage she had no chance to mention to him that they wanted to renew their lease for another six months at an increased rental on condition that they could have the use of the pottery as well. Mr. Knight was a keen amateur painter, and now that he had retired was going to pursue what had been a hobby in earnest. He had been using one of the bedrooms in the cottage as a studio, but he needed more light now that the days were short and proposed to work in the pottery.

This would mean clearing the place of the stuff stored there by Anna and Ricky, and would necessitate her consulting him about it. She was reluctant to ring him at the office where he wouldn't be able to talk freely, so after trying the number of his flat several times without success she decided to write to him. In her letter she told him that she had decided to let the pottery to her tenants and mentioned that since Jeremy was away at school she thought of going down to St. Aurryns for the weekend and wondered if he would care to join her at the hotel as she was sure Mrs. Brayle would be able to put them up.

'Perhaps we could make some combined arrangements about storage,' she wrote, 'which would work out cheaper than two separate undertakings. Anyway, we can discuss that when I see you.'

The following evening Sara was later than usual, and Anna was beginning to feel anxious when she heard a key in the door and the next minute found herself confronted with Drewe's stepsister, white with fury.

'How dare you!' hissed the other girl, tearing off her coat and flinging it down on a chair. 'How dare you go behind my back to Ricky, writing to him and suggesting that he joins you for a weekend in Cornwall!'

Anna was taken completely aback. It

had never occurred to her that Sara would misinterpret her action. She'd taken it for granted that Ricky would want to see to the disposal of his own goods which were probably quite valuable, and the simplest arrangement had seemed for them both to be in Cornwall at the same time.

'I'm sorry if I've upset you, Sara, it's just that Ricky and I are such old friends that I didn't think you'd object to my writing to him.'

'You must be joking. You know that we're in love and yet you calmly suggest that he spends a weekend in Cornwall with you. There was no mention of my coming too; were you hoping that he'd fob me off with some excuse?'

'Certainly not. This is purely a matter of business.'

'I'm sure it is. I'm neither blind nor stupid, you know. I'm aware that you've always wanted him; this is just an excuse to get him to yourself in the hope of cutting me out.'

'You're quite wrong,' protested Anna,

but she might as well have saved her breath. Without another word Sara snatched up her coat and rushed up the stairs, the slam of her bedroom door echoing through the house.

Anna remained where she was, standing quite still for a long, pain-filled minute. Was it true that her underlying motive for writing to Ricky had been the hope of ultimately winning him back? If so, she'd been quite unconscious of it, but now she felt so numb and bewildered that she wasn't sure of anything any more except the fact that if Sara's accusation wasn't to be justified she must put him out of her heart and mind completely.

Ricky rang the next morning, and for the first time she wasn't delighted to hear his voice.

'How are relations between you and Sara?' he asked. 'She left here in a fine temper last night and I don't suppose it improved on the journey.'

'It didn't,' admitted Anna wryly. 'I'm afraid when I wrote that letter I made a mistake, but I didn't expect her to jump to the wrong conclusion.'

'She wouldn't have seen the letter if it hadn't been for the fact that the post didn't arrive before I left for the office, and when I returned to the flat last evening Sara was with me. She picked up the letter, saw the postmark, and guessing it was from you demanded to read it. I tried to explain the situation, but, well, you saw how she reacted.'

'It was stupid of me not to realise how it would look to her. I'm sorry, Ricky.'

'Well, it rules out any chance of our meeting in Cornwall. Do you really have to clear the pottery, Anna? It will be a confounded nuisance having to make fresh arrangements for my stuff.'

'I think I must let the Knights take possession, but I'll ring Mrs. Brayle and see if she could help.'

'Oh, all right,' said Ricky carelessly. 'I'll leave it to you.'

Mrs. Brayle proved as obliging as ever, and said that for the time being the contents of the pottery could be stored in the hotel cellar.

'It's quite dry down there and I'll see the furniture's covered up. Tom Holcombe will transport everything in his van.'

'It's very good of you,' said Anna gratefully. 'I'll send you a cheque.'

'I should have thought that Ricky Beeston could have come down and seen to this business for you. After all, most of the stuff is his.'

'He's pretty tied up at the moment,' Anna defended him quickly.

'And what about you; are you settling down in Sussex?'

'I'm leading a very pleasant life with plenty of leisure while Jeremy's away at school.'

'Don't forget that I can always squeeze you in any time you want to come down here.'

'Thank you for the invitation and for all your kindness.'

That accomplished Anna was left to devise some means of soothing Sara.

They couldn't continue to live in the same house in a state of open hostility so she would have to make the first move. Deciding that the sooner she got it over the better she tackled Sara when the girl came home that evening.

'Sara,' she said resolutely, 'I'm sorry if my letter to Ricky upset you but I really didn't intend it to so can you manage to forget it? It's going to make the house very uncomfortable if we're at odds with each other.'

'It's a pity you didn't think of that earlier.'

'Perhaps it is,' agreed Anna quietly, 'but couldn't we behave reasonably towards each other? It won't be for very long.'

'Very well,' said Sara grudgingly. 'I suppose I can manage that,' and at dinner that evening she made several allusions to her modelling course instead of sitting in a sullen silence or making sarcastic remarks which were intended to annoy. Anna followed her lead, and the evening passed with less strain than might have been expected.

Jeremy was having his exeat that Saturday and Anna had arranged to pick him up at school and take him out. He reminded her about having lunch in the village and mentioned that there was a farmhouse a few miles away where they served teas with cream and strawberry jam so Anna rang up and booked a table at the Fairacre Arms after asking Sara what kind of a pattern had been followed on these occasions.

'Oh, they stuff themselves with food and go to the cinema if there's a decent film on.'

'What shall I wear? I don't want to let Jeremy down but on the other hand I don't want to be overdressed. I've got a dark green suit with a beaver collar and a matching beaver cap.'

'That sounds all right.'

The car was polished and Anna set off on a crisp autumn morning which gave promise of being a sunny day. It took her about an hour and a half to reach the school which stood in its own grounds on the outskirts of a pleasant village. The entrance gates stood open, and the boys had posted themselves on either side of the winding drive so that they could greet the parents and friends who had come to take them out.

Jeremy was stationed near the house, his face beaming as he rushed forward and guided Anna into a convenient spot for parking.

'Gosh, I thought you'd never come,' he cried. 'Did you have a good journey?'

'Yes,' Anna told him, 'but it took a little longer than I expected because I wasn't sure of the way. What do we do now?'

'I have to tell Matron that I'm going out. Do you want to come along too?'

'Would you like me to? I shouldn't care to do the wrong thing.'

'Most mothers go to see her and you look all right in that fur hat.'

Taking this to be the highest form of praise Anna accompanied him to the Matron who beamed approvingly and hoped they would have a nice day. Then they drove down to the village, and Jeremy showed her the old Market Cross and the Norman church with its Saxon font and the leper's squint by the altar.

Lunch at the Fairacre Arms was a cheerful affair since the dining-room was full of boys from the school with their parents. Jeremy ate enormously, and chattered away about his form master and his friends. Anna was glad to see that he seemed happy and had quite got over his home-sickness, and when he couldn't eat even one more chocolate mint with his coffee she said: 'Well, what's the programme now?'

'There's a western on at the cinema in Cherminster. Could we go to see that?'

Suppressing a shudder Anna replied that she thought they could so off they went to Cherminster where Jeremy spent a blissful couple of hours watching Indians fighting cowboys and cowboys fighting each other. Then they ate scones, cream and jam at the farmhouse Jeremy had previously mentioned, and finally she drove him back to school.

'Gosh, it's been a super day,' declared Jeremy as they drew up outside.

'I'm glad,' answered Anna. 'I've enjoyed it too.'

'You'll still be here at half term and at Christmas, won't you?'

'I'm not quite sure. It will depend on your step-brother.'

'Then I'll write and ask him not to let you go.'

Jeremy cast a quick look round, and as there was no one in sight he gave her a hug before running into school. She stared after him, loving him as much as if he were her own. She would miss him dreadfully when she had to leave Heathlands, but she wouldn't think about that yet.

She was tired by the end of her journey and wanted nothing so much as a bath and to put her feet up. The bath was soon accomplished, and after it she slipped into a caftan of dark blue wool. Mrs. Mabledon was in the kitchen and eager to hear the latest news of Jeremy.

'He's settling down very well, judging by his appetite,' Anna told her. 'He seemed to enjoy his day and so did I apart from the film. I was bored to death by that, and would have fallen asleep twice if it hadn't been so noisy.'

'I can't bear westerns either,' said Mrs. Mabledon. 'I was wondering if you'd like to have your dinner on a tray. I expect you're tired, and Sara isn't in. She came downstairs just after you left and said she'd be out all day. She must have been in a mighty hurry because the next thing I knew she'd gone.'

'Oh,' said Anna. 'I suppose she and Ricky are spending the evening together. In that case I will have my dinner on a tray and I'll probably have an early night.'

She ate her dinner, watched a television play, and wondered how late Sara was likely to be. She didn't want to go to bed before the girl was in but was feeling reluctant to stay up much longer when Mrs. Mabledon burst into the room, her face expressing alarm.

'I've just been into Sara's room to fetch a dress she asked me to send to the cleaners,' she said, 'and I found this.'

She held out an envelope with 'Anna' scrawled across it and Anna took it from her, ripping it open to read the single sheet it contained.

'Is it important?' asked Mrs. Mabledon anxiously. 'I meant to collect that dress this morning but I forgot all about it until a moment ago.'

'I don't think it would have made any difference when you'd found this note. The damage is done. Sara and Ricky are married.'

'Oh no!' cried Mrs. Mabledon. 'How could she do such a thing when Mr. Drewe told her she must wait a year. Whatever will he say?'

'A great deal, I should imagine,' returned Anna. Once more she read the half-dozen lines which gave the news that

Sara and Ricky were getting married at a registry office early that morning and going away for the weekend.

'We'll be back tomorrow evening,' Sara had written, 'because neither of us is flush with money, also I want to collect my things and take them to Ricky's flat.'

Anna passed the note to Mrs. Mabledon and the older woman read it, then shook her head.

'The foolish girl, what does she know about running a flat? I only hope she doesn't live to rue this day. I see now why she slipped out so quickly this morning. She must have had some luggage with her.'

She went back to the kitchen, plainly upset, and Anna stood with the note crumpled in her hand, knowing that she would have to get in touch with Drewe Chatham and dreading the thought of it. She had the telephone number of his hotel in Brussels to be used only in an emergency which this certainly was, and she forced herself to go to the telephone and ask for it. The operator said there was an hour's delay on calls to the Continent so Anna sat there, tense with apprehension, until when at last the telephone did ring she jumped up in a flurry.

It was the impersonal voice of the hotel receptionist, and fortunately Anna's French proved adequate because in a few moments Drewe Chatham's deep, impatient voice was saying: 'Yes, who is it?'

'It's Anna Blakeney,' answered Anna, trying to keep her own voice steady.

'Is something wrong?'

'Sara went out after breakfast and we've just found a note in her bedroom informing us that she and Ricky were getting married this morning.'

There was a pause and Anna waited for the blast.

Her employer said: 'The damned stupid little idiot,' in a tone of intense exasperation and then: 'Don't worry, I'll be home as soon as I can get a seat on a plane.'

'If it means you postponing an important meeting or anything like that I can cope,' said Anna. 'In her note Sara says that they'll be calling at Heathlands tomorrow night to pick up her things so she hasn't disappeared into the blue. It was just that I thought you ought to know what had happened.'

'Of course. Expect me sometime tomorrow. Anything else?'

'No, nothing. Goodbye.'

Anna's hand was trembling as she replaced the receiver though she couldn't have said why she felt so nervous. What did she expect Mr. Chatham to do — abuse her over the telephone for not having taken better care of Sara? No one could have guessed that the girl would defy her stepbrother, but the old feeling of guilt at having introduced Sara to Ricky nagged at her. If only the Chathams had stayed in a different Cornish hotel this summer what a lot of sorrow everyone would have been spared.

The next day seemed to drag out

interminably, and Anna couldn't settle to anything. She half hoped that her employer wouldn't be able to get a seat on a plane so that Sara and Ricky could call at Heathlands and be away again before he arrived, but that would only postpone the confrontation. As it happened he arrived about half past two, and when she heard his car come to a stop outside the front door Anna felt quite unable to move for a moment. Then she braced herself as his key grated in the lock and he banged the door behind him.

She came forward into the hall and said: 'I'm truly sorry, Mr. Chatham, to have to bring you home a second time. I never thought Sara would do a thing like this.'

'Didn't you?' he answered dryly. 'I was afraid of it all along only I hoped Beeston would have more sense. I suppose Sara thought it would be romantic to have a secret wedding, but she'll have a rude awakening when she tries to keep house on Beeston's salary.'

He shot a keen glance at her and said: 'You look very pale. Did you get any sleep last night?'

'Not much,' confessed Anna. 'I lay awake for hours wishing I'd kept a better eye on Sara.'

'Why? I didn't install you here to be her gaoler. You couldn't be expected to watch her every hour of the day.'

The relief was so great that Anna felt the tears well up. She swallowed hard to subdue her emotion, but it was no use. The strain of the last few weeks coupled with her sleepless night overwhelmed her, and she found herself weeping in spite of all her efforts to calm herself. The more she tried to stop the harder she cried, and she was scarcely aware of Drewe Chatham's arm coming round her until a large handkerchief was pressed into her hand.

'Mop them up with that,' he advised gently. 'You'll soon feel better.'

Anna gulped, and gradually gained control of herself.

'I'm sorry, I've never made such an

exhibition of myself before,' she quavered, and then realised to her horror that his arm was still encircling her and that she was leaning her head against his shoulder. She jerked herself upright immediately, and his arm dropped to his side.

'Don't be too hard on yourself,' he said. 'Your parents were killed in that accident as well as my father and stepmother, and I don't imagine you've really recovered from the shock of it yet. Also this marriage of Sara's has complications too. Beeston was your friend before he was hers, and that wouldn't make things easier for you.'

'No,' admitted Anna desolately.

That was what had been weighing so heavily on her all day. It wasn't only the prospect of her employer's anger, it was the bleak knowledge that now Ricky was lost to her for ever.

5

Drewe Chatham left the room and returned in a moment with a glass containing brandy in his hand.

'Drink that,' he ordered, 'and then go and lie down for an hour. You'll probably fall asleep which will do you good.'

Anna drank the brandy without protest and then went up to her room, conscious of her swollen eyes. Some people might be able to cry without making themselves positively plain but she certainly wasn't one of them, she thought with a grimace, as she caught sight of her reflection in the mirror of the dressing table. She slipped out of her dress and shoes to lie down on the bed and pulling the eiderdown over her promptly fell asleep. She wakened a couple of hours later feeling very much better, and having tidied herself went downstairs to the drawing-room.

There was no sign of her employer so she made herself a pot of tea in the kitchen since Mrs. Mabledon had gone out. She decided to drink it there and was taking a cup and saucer out of the cupboard when the door opened and Drewe Chatham appeared.

'Good,' he said. 'I was just feeling like a cup of tea. Is there enough for two in that pot?'

'Yes, ample,' answered Anna. 'Where will you have it, in the drawing-room or your study?'

'Why not here? Are there any biscuits?'

He sounded so like Jeremy that she couldn't help smiling, and he smiled back.

'That's better. Did you manage to fall asleep?'

'I did, and it's made all the difference.'

Anna poured out the tea and found the biscuits. They both sat down at the kitchen table and she said: 'I haven't had time to tell you that I went down to the school yesterday to take Jeremy out. He seemed to enjoy himself; at all events, he ate enough for six. We had lunch at the Fairacre Arms in the village.'

'And after that?'

'I endured two hours of boredom at the cinema. What is it that boys find so fascinating about cowboys and Indians?'

Drewe Chatham grinned. 'Poor you. I always preferred thrillers myself. Has Jeremy settled down at school?'

'Yes. He wanted me to promise that I'd still be here when he came home at Christmas.'

'That's not surprising. His world having been turned upside down once he's obviously terrified of another upheaval. That's why I want you to stay on until he's regained his confidence. I don't imagine that will take very long. Children are remarkably resilient.'

'I'll stay on as long as you wish,' Anna found herself saying, rather to her own surprise. Only a short while ago she'd been convinced that she'd made a mistake in coming to Heathlands; now she realised how reluctant she'd be to leave it. Of course that was because she'd grown so attached to Jeremy, she assured herself.

'Then you don't find it boring here while Jeremy's at school?'

'Not in the least, but I do feel guilty at taking a salary which I'm not really earning. Isn't there anything I could do for you while I've got so much free time? I'm a competent typist.'

'Are you? Then there are a couple of letters you could type for me. I intended to go up to the office tomorrow and have them done there, but if you could manage them then I could ring up instead and drive straight to Heathrow.'

'I can do them as soon as you like.'

'No need to leap up right away, there's plenty of time.'

As he tilted his chair back and took another biscuit Anna was conscious of his relaxed mood. She was suddenly aware of the tan of his skin against his white shirt collar and wondered how he occupied himself at the weekends while he was away. It was more than likely that he was entertained by his business colleagues and probably some of them had attractive daughters.

As if he were aware of her scrutiny he turned his head and looked full at her. She felt her colour rise and then there was the sound of a door closing and Mrs. Mabledon walked into the kitchen. She took in the teapot, together with the open biscuit tin and said reproachfully: 'You don't usually care for afternoon tea, Mr. Drewe, otherwise I'd have set the trolley for you. To think of you using the kitchen cups!'

'What does that matter?' he countered amusedly. 'Miss Blakeney wanted to give me my tea in state in the drawing-room but it tastes just the same in here.'

'That's as may be but I'll ask you to

remove yourself to the drawing-room now or you won't get any dinner tonight,' said Mrs. Mabledon firmly, and shooed them both out.

'Would you like me to type those letters for you now?' asked Anna.

'Yes, please. Come along to the study. There's a portable there. Can you do shorthand?'

'Yes, though I'm not very fast.'

Once more he was completely business-like in his approach and he dictated two letters clearly and concisely. Anna typed them, and when they were ready he thanked her absently with his head bent over a mass of figures. She went quietly out of the room, conscious of an absurd sense of deflation. For a short while she'd seen him as a man as well as a rather forbidding employer, but now they were back on the old footing.

Sara and Ricky arrived about six, Ricky's car chugging up to the front door. Anna heard it and went to meet them so that she could warn Sara of her stepbrother's return.

Sara's face reflected her dismay.

Ricky put his arm protectively round his wife's shoulders. 'Well, never mind. We only have to face him once.'

Sara tossed her head defiantly. 'Yes, of course. Anyway, we're married and nothing he can say or do will alter that.'

She marched inside the house, but as the door of the study was shut and Drewe showed no sign of emerging her militant air was wasted. In the drawing-room she flopped into a chair and demanded aggressively: 'Was Drewe furious when he heard the news?'

'Not nearly as much as I expected,' said Anna frankly. 'He took it quite calmly. Where are you going to live?'

'In Ricky's flat. The other two men have moved out and as most of the furniture was theirs we'll have to acquire some. I think Drewe ought to let me take several pieces from here. After all, they belonged to Mummy and Daddy so they must have been left to Jeremy and me.'

She shifted restlessly. 'Is Drewe going

to stay in the study all night?'

'He was working on some figures,' said Anna, adding tactfully: 'He probably hasn't realised you're here.'

'Of course he has. He's doing this on purpose and I shall go and rout him out.'

Anna guessed that she wasn't feeling as confident as she sounded, but at least she had the courage to walk across the hall and open the study door.

Anna was left alone with Ricky who said ruefully: 'Can you forgive me for letting you in for all this? It couldn't have been pleasant for you to have to break the news to Drewe, but to slip away and get married seemed the only solution to our problem.'

'But couldn't you have waited until the year was up, Ricky? It would have made things so much easier for everyone.'

'Maybe, but Sara was convinced that her stepbrother was deliberately setting out to make things as difficult as possible for us in the hope of parting us, and I think she was right. In any case, she was so unhappy that I had to give in though I didn't want to be married in such a furtive way.'

Anna looked troubled. 'It won't be easy starting married life on your income after what Sara's been used to.'

'No, but she's hoping that Drewe will make her an allowance. After all, he won't be keeping her, and under the terms of her father's will her share of his estate is left in trust for her until she's twenty-one.'

Naturally he and Sara had discussed the matter thoroughly, but Anna couldn't help being surprised at the business-like manner in which he spoke of it to her. She was saved from having to reply by Sara coming out of the study and saying: 'Ricky, Drewe wants a word with you.'

Ricky rose and left the room while Sara sat down on the arm of a chair and fiddled restlessly with an ashtray on the small table near her. Her aggressiveness had subsided, and she said suddenly: 'Drewe's taken it better than I expected.

I thought he would have flung me out into the snow.'

'He's much too civilised for that,' said Anna. 'What about the modelling course? Do you intend to carry on with that?'

'I might as well. I'll have to do something all day while Ricky's at the office, and if I'm offered any engagements at the end of it the money will come in useful. Drewe's going to transfer a block of shares into my name so that I shall draw the interest on them, and I'm to have some of the furniture from here for the flat so that we ought to be able to make it comfortable. Of course as soon as Ricky gets promotion I want to move to a better neighbourhood. I'd like one of those little mews houses with a scarlet front door and a bay tree in a tub on either side of it.'

'In the meantime are you and Ricky staying to dinner because if so I ought to tell Mrs. Mabledon.'

'Oh, we're counting on having dinner

here. There'll be nothing in the flat if we go back there, and we've used most of our spare money during the last couple of days.'

Mrs. Mabledon had automatically catered for two extra, and had a basket of food ready for Sara when they left.

'This will keep you going until you've time to do some shopping,' she said.

When they'd gone Anna felt quite numb. The worst was over, their marriage was a reality, and now she had to start to live her own life again. She went up to bed expecting to spend another sleepless night, but to her surprise she slept well and woke feeling refreshed.

Drewe Chatham was already eating breakfast when she went down and he said: 'I'm off to Brussels again today but I shall be back in a couple of weeks. My fiancée is due home then from her trip and she'll be coming down here for the weekend, I hope. As I expect Sara and Ricky will be here too the house will be fairly full. Do you think you'll be able to cope?'

'Of course,' answered Anna. 'Sara was telling me how generous you'd been to her. I think she appreciated it.'

'Since nothing can alter the fact that she's married I want her to have the opportunity to make a success of it. I don't think she's going to find it quite so easy to run a flat as she imagines so keep an eye on her, will you?'

'Certainly, if she'll let me.'

'She may be glad to. I'm not impressed with Beeston. I suspect his motives.'

Anna flushed. 'I'm sure you're misjudging him.'

'I forgot you know him so much better than I do,' returned Drewe Chatham smoothly and, she was sure, sarcastically.

Sara and Ricky came over to Heathlands the next weekend, Sara declaring frankly that the housekeeping allowance Ricky had given her didn't stretch nearly far enough.

'Food's so expensive,' she exclaimed, 'and Ricky's got an enormous appetite.'

'That's an exaggeration,' he retorted, 'but I do expect a decent meal when I get home at nights. After all, I only snatch a sandwich at midday.'

'I don't always have time for that and then when I get home at night tired out you expect me to cook. It would be much more convenient for us to eat out in the evenings.'

'We simply can't afford it every night.'

'It's such a bore to be short of money,' sighed Sara. 'As soon as I've finished my course I'm going all out to earn as much as I can.'

'Roll on the day,' said Ricky cheerfully. 'It's a lovely evening. Are you coming out for a walk?'

Sara shook her head. 'Not tonight, I'm too tired. You go.'

'I think I will just for half an hour.'

Ricky disappeared, and Sara curled up in one of the big armchairs.

'Drewe doesn't believe in Ricky,' she

said, 'but I know he's going to get on. It won't be long before we're out of that flat and into something much better.'

'I'm sure it won't,' agreed Anna, 'but in the meantime what do you think about asking Mrs. Mabledon to show you a few simple dishes? That kind of knowledge always comes in useful.'

'I suppose so,' agreed Sara unenthusiastically. 'All right, she can give me some hints tomorrow. By the way, did Drewe say anything to you about Althea coming home?'

'Before he left he did mention that his fiancée would be spending the weekend here in about a fortnight,' said Anna cautiously.

'I guessed she'd soon be back in England. I wonder when the wedding will take place. There can't be any reason now for them to delay it.'

Anna wondered the same thing herself. If Drewe Chatham intended to marry in the near future and bring his bride to live at Heathlands then there certainly wouldn't be any necessity for her to stay on. She hoped that his wife would be kind to Jeremy. It wouldn't be easy starting married life with a young stepbrother in the house, but Jeremy needed love and affection and to feel that he was wanted.

In the middle of the week there was a letter from her employer to say that he expected to be back in England on Thursday and that he and Miss Lymington would be coming down to Heathlands on the Friday evening in time for dinner.

'And Sara and her husband will be here as well so that means five for dinner,' said Mrs. Mabledon. 'I'd better roast a nice sirloin. Mr. Drewe always enjoys that, and if Miss Lymington's been round the world she'll have had her fill of foreign food.'

'What's she like?' asked Anna, busily polishing silver.

'Oh, a brunette,' answered Mrs. Mabledon. 'Dark glossy hair and big brown eyes. Not that I've seen much of her because she's been down here very little. I had the impression that she didn't care for the country so I don't know how she'll settle to life in this house. I always understood that she and Mr. Drewe were going to have a flat in town.'

'Oh, I see.'

Jeremy wouldn't enjoy the holidays nearly so much without the pool in the garden and his walks in the woods, but perhaps Miss Lymington would be willing to go on living at Heathlands for a few years particularly if she should have a family of her own to bring up. Anna discovered that she could quite easily imagine Drewe Chatham in the role of a father. She thought that he would stand no nonsense from his children, but respect them as individuals and try to see their point of view.

'We'd better get Sara's old room ready for her while Sara and Ricky occupy the spare room,' suggested Anna.

She took a lot of trouble to make the

bedroom as attractive as possible with flowers and new magazines and a box of biscuits on the bedside table. She wondered why her employer was bringing his fiancée down here on her first weekend back in England. If she weren't fond of the country it seemed likely that she would have preferred to remain in town where she could have him to herself.

It was around six when the black car swept through the gates, and Anna swallowed her apprehension as she went forward to greet the visitor. Althea Lymington wasn't more than average height, but she had a beautifully proportioned figure and her cashmere slacks and sweater in a warm honey colour topped by a jacket of exactly toning suede fitted her perfectly. As Mrs. Mabledon had said she was dark, but her shoulder-length hair had a coppery sheen where the light fell on it and her brown eyes were the colour of sherry. There was no warmth in them, however, or in the smile which curved her lips mechanically when she was introduced to Anna.

'So you're the girl who's been looking after Jeremy,' she remarked. 'I imagine he's rather a handful.'

'Not really,' replied Anna. 'He's not a saint but he's a very reasonable boy and we get on well together.'

'How fortunate,' said Althea Lymington perfunctorily. She turned to Drewe. 'Darling, you'll have to amuse yourself while I take a bath. I feel absolutely filthy after that drive from town.'

'I'll be in the study looking over some papers until you're ready,' he answered.

Althea moved to the stairs, saying over her shoulder: 'Will you ask someone to bring my cases up?'

'I'll bring them,' and Anna moved to pick them up but Drewe Chatham forestalled her.

'They're too heavy for you so I'll carry them if you'll lead the way to Althea's room.'

'I've put Miss Lymington in Sara's

old room,' said Anna. 'It gets the morning sun and there's a bathroom next door.'

'I can't understand why your father didn't have more bathrooms put in, Drewe,' commented Althea. 'Two to six bedrooms is ridiculous; I should certainly need another one at least.'

'That's one of the reasons why I wanted you to come down this weekend so that we could discuss possible alterations. We could do with extra garage space too so it might be an idea to build onto the existing garage and run a bathroom out over the top.'

'Yes, that sounds feasible. Daddy knows a very good architect, an up and coming young man. I'll get him to put you in touch.'

Aware that they'd forgotten she existed Anna slipped away to set the dining table for dinner and it was while she was doing it that Sara and Ricky arrived.

Sara said: 'I suppose she's here, I saw the car,' and Anna answered: 'If you mean Miss Lymington she's upstairs having a bath.'

Sara grimaced. 'And then she'll sweep in to dinner looking like a fashion plate, hoping to outdo everyone else.'

Anna understood what Sara meant when Althea made her appearance at dinner. She was wearing a caftan in a subtle shade of coral pink interwoven with a gold thread so that the material shimmered when she moved. Her hair had been piled on top of her head in a sleek coil augmented with a hair piece, and this coupled with the chandelier earrings in gold filigree which she wore, made her neck look very long and slender. Beside her Anna felt plain and uninteresting in a simple black dress with a ruffle of white at the neck, but she reflected ruefully that it couldn't be expected to have the same impact as the caftan which had cost at least five times as much.

The sirloin was one of Mrs. Mabledon's triumphs, rare and juicy, but

Althea accepted only a tiny helping of meat and refused both potatoes and the featherlight Yorkshire pudding. Anna, having worked hard all day with only a snack lunch, was hungry and thoroughly enjoyed the meal. Althea raised her eyebrows when the other girl took a portion of raspberry mousse served with whipped cream.

'Aren't you afraid of putting on pounds eating puddings like that?' she remarked sweetly.

To Anna's surprise before she could reply Drewe Chatham said: 'I don't think Miss Blakeney's any need to bother about watching her weight or you either, Althea.'

'Darling, you don't know what you're talking about. You wouldn't like to see me fat and shapeless, would you?'

'I can't believe there's any danger of that.'

'No, because I'm constantly on my guard.'

Drewe Chatham's mouth tightened and then relaxed, and for a second

Althea's eyes narrowed. Then she laughed lightly.

'This conversation's getting boring; let's change it. Sara, how are you finding married life?'

'She can thoroughly recommend it, can't you, Sara?' interposed Ricky easily. 'I know I can.'

Althea smiled at him. 'Yes, I can see that you're weathering it well.'

'We both are,' confirmed Sara quickly. 'It's fun.'

'I'm so glad,' said Althea sweetly. 'I must come and see your flat. Where exactly is it?'

'At the top of a rather seedy house in Earls Court,' declared Ricky, while Sara added: 'But we shan't be staying there long. I'm looking out for somewhere else.'

'I might be able to help you,' said Althea. 'A friend of a friend of mine wants to sublet a small flat for a year. She's going abroad and she isn't so much concerned with asking a high rent as letting it to careful tenants who will get out without fuss when she needs it again. I'll give her a ring when she's back in town. I know she won't be doing anything about it just yet.'

Sara's face lit up. 'Oh, would you, Althea? It sounds as if it might be exactly what we want.'

The conversation ebbed and flowed, but not much of it came Anna's way. Five was an awkward number round a dinner table, and subtly Althea Lymington made her feel very much the odd one out. When the meal was over, knowing that there would be a lot of clearing up to do in the kitchen, Anna went to bring in the coffee, and when she sat down again in the drawing-room behind the tray she saw Althea's brows lift fractionally as if she thought Anna ought to have stayed in the kitchen with Mrs. Mabledon.

Althea talked amusingly about her recent trip and then all at once she jumped up and pulling back the curtains from the long french windows said: 'It's a beautiful night. Drewe, wouldn't you like to show me the garden by moonlight?'

'Of course,' he said, rising, and when he'd unlatched the long window she slipped her arm through his and drew him into the garden.

'Why don't we follow their example?' said Ricky and he and Sara stepped outside, leaving Anna alone.

She hadn't enjoyed the evening so far but now she felt completely isolated. Deciding that she'd no intention of sitting there until they came back she collected the coffee cups and carried the tray into the kitchen.

Mrs. Mabledon was sitting with her feet up, the dishwasher rattling away with its load, and she said: 'Did they enjoy the meal? I notice most of the sirloin disappeared. There's just about enough left for a cottage pie. Mr. Drewe loves one of those with plenty of onion.'

'The beef melted in the mouth,' Anna assured her, 'and so did the Yorkshire pudding. You must show me how to make one like that. Mine always come out much more solid.'

'It's a knack,' said Mrs. Mabledon, looking gratified. 'What are they all doing now?'

'They've gone into the garden to enjoy the moonlight.'

'It is a lovely night. It's a pity you haven't got someone to take you outside to gaze at the moon. I'm past it myself. Give me a good cup of tea and a nice book in preference any day.'

Anna laughed. 'You sound as if you don't regret having reached that stage.'

'I don't,' said Mrs. Mabledon frankly. 'I've had my moments, but it was all a long time ago and now I'll settle for comfort. However, there's no reason why you should. You're young and all your life's before you.'

'I suppose so,' said Anna ruefully, 'but there's not much likelihood of anything exciting happening in the near future.'

Not even a walk in the moonlight, she told herself, as she started to climb the stairs, but halfway up them she paused and then descended again. She felt too restless to go to bed. If she did she wouldn't sleep and she longed for a breath of fresh air. She crossed the hall and then quietly opened the front door and stepped out into the garden. A faint breeze sighed through the trees, and looking up she saw the moon riding high and casting a silvery radiance over everything. She walked slowly round the side of the house towards the rose garden, guessing that Sara and Ricky would be by the pool but keeping a wary eye out for Drewe Chatham and his fiancée.

In the shadow of the wall which cut off the kitchen garden she paused, relaxing in the peace of the evening, then she moved away and as she did so a figure detached itself from further along the wall and her heart leaped into her throat as she jerked back.

'It's all right,' a voice said. 'I'm sorry if I startled you,' and her employer emerged from the shadow.

'I didn't know there was anyone else here,' Anna gasped, and wondered what had happened to Althea Lymington.

As if he'd read her thoughts Drewe Chatham said: 'Althea thought the ground was damp so she's gone inside but I stayed to finish my cigarette. Have one?'

'Thank you. I don't often smoke, but — '

'You need one to steady your nerves. It was stupid of me not to realise you couldn't see me.'

They stood there side by side in a companionable silence until Anna said: 'You know, I'm rather sorry that men have landed on the moon. I've always liked to think of it as remote and inaccessible.'

'Artemis, the Moon goddess, as opposed to dust-filled craters,' he remarked amusedly.

'Well, why not? When all the illusions have vanished life's a very grim affair.'

'You know, Miss Blakeney, I never suspected you of being a romantic,' he said mockingly.

Out here in the moonlight everything seemed slightly unreal and Anna was seized with recklessness.

'But then you don't really know much about me,' she riposted.

'I'm beginning to think I don't,' he answered slowly, and he moved to face her.

All of a sudden there was tension between them, but before it could build up there was the click of heels on the path and Althea appeared.

'Drewe,' she protested, 'aren't you coming inside? I don't enjoy playing gooseberry to Sara and her husband. Oh!'

As she spoke she caught sight of Anna and her tone altered subtly.

'Are you enjoying the moonlight too, Miss Blakeney? I thought you'd gone to bed.'

'I found the atmosphere stuffy so I decided to have a breath of air.'

'How remarkable. I found it quite chilly out here. Drewe, are you coming?'

Anna didn't wait to hear him answer. She said quickly: 'Good night,' and walked away as rapidly as she could. Once in her room she stared at herself in the mirror, trying to cool her cheeks. It was quite obvious that Althea thought she'd deliberately waylaid Drewe Chatham in the garden, and her suspicions weren't going to improve relations between them.

It seemed quite likely that they were responsible for her early appearance at breakfast the next morning, and she made it clear from the start that Drewe wouldn't have any chance to stray that day.

'You don't mind if we go off and leave you to amuse yourselves, do you?' she asked Sara smilingly. 'It's such ages since Drewe and I were alone together. We shall have lunch at our favourite inn and spend a thoroughly lazy day.'

Evidently this programme met with her fiancé's approval because the two of them set off soon after breakfast, Althea announcing gaily that they wouldn't be back until dinner. Sara and Ricky lounged about the house, and then after lunch Ricky sought Anna out in the garden where she was gathering chrysanthemums.

'I thought I might as well pick these in case we have a heavy frost,' she said. 'Where's Sara?'

'Washing and setting her hair. I hope Althea can do something for us with regard to that flat. It's pretty crummy where we are. I didn't seem to notice it so much sharing with two men, but when Sara's involved it's different.'

'You're not regretting having married her so quickly?'

'Good Lord, no,' denied Ricky instantly, 'but I'm not altogether happy about my job.'

'Your job? But I thought the prospects were so good.'

'In general they may be, but the fact is I prefer working with people rather than figures. Chatham Exports may be efficient but it's so damned impersonal.'

'What a pity you didn't realise that before,' said Anna. 'You might have done better to remain in interior decorating.'

'I might at that. Hilary could be maddening but at least she was human. Still, not to worry. I expect it will all work out in the end. How are things with you, Anna? Any plans for the future yet?'

'I shall be staying on here until Mr. Chatham marries, but after that — '

'I don't imagine he'll hesitate long before tying himself up. Althea's certainly luscious, isn't she, and I understand her father's rolling in money.'

The way Ricky spoke jarred on Anna, and she answered him more sharply than she intended. 'I don't believe that would weigh with Mr. Chatham at all.'

Ricky said in surprise: 'I thought you didn't like him.'

'I don't particularly, but it doesn't seem fair to label him mercenary without any justification.'

'You're very quick to fly to his defence. Don't tell me that you've fallen for him,' said Ricky with a grin.

'Don't be ridiculous,' answered Anna shortly.

He put his hand on her arm. 'Sorry, I was only teasing. Now I suppose I'd better go and see what my wife's doing but if you should hear of any congenial openings let me know, will you?'

'Of course, but I'm hardly likely to.'

When he'd gone back to the house she paused in her flower cutting. So Ricky didn't like his job and was on the lookout for another. Perhaps he'd found things difficult since he'd married Sara. It was rather an awkward position to be in — one of the junior staff yet married to the Managing Director's sister — but surely he ought to have been prepared for that. She wished there was something she could do to help but couldn't think of anything. Drewe Chatham was the only person she could approach and she could scarcely ask this particular favour of him.

Drewe and Althea arrived home about six, and Althea waxed lyrical over dinner about the country inn where they'd had lunch.

'It was perfect,' she enthused, 'completely unspoilt, and after the meal we drank our coffee in the garden on a little terrace sheltered by those old brick walls which hold all the sun. Darling, we must go there again very soon.'

'Yes, it is a nice spot,' agreed Drewe. 'Jeremy would enjoy it too. Next time he's home you and I will take him over there, Miss Blakeney.'

Althea pouted. 'I thought it was to be our special place.'

'We could hardly expect to keep it quite to ourselves,' said Drewe Chatham lightly. 'By the way, Althea, I must go over some papers for an hour after dinner if you'll excuse me. Miss Blakeney, could you transcribe some notes for me? I've made a series of almost undecipherable jottings and I'd like to have them typed out while I can still read them.'

'Certainly,' said Anna, and Althea put her hand on Drewe's arm at the same time smiling into his eyes.

'Darling, you're not going to work tonight when we haven't seen each other for so long.'

'I'm afraid I must. There are some very important negotiations in the offing, and I need to be thoroughly conversant with these statistics. After all, we've spent the whole of today together so I don't really think you can accuse me of neglecting you.'

'I'm not accusing you of anything, it's just that naturally I want to be with you as much as I can.'

'I shan't be more than an hour. Ready, Miss Blakeney? We'll have our coffee in the study.'

Althea said no more but for a second there was an ugly twist to her mouth, then she smiled and said: 'All right, you bully, but if you don't emerge in an hour I shall come and drag you out.'

Mrs. Mabledon brought coffee into the study, and Anna set to work on the notes. Her employer was right, they were hard to read, but she struggled on and in the end managed to decipher them. When she'd finished Drewe Chatham looked her typescript over, and then said approvingly : 'Good girl, that's set things out a lot more clearly. You can go back to the drawing-room now.'

'Are you sure there's nothing more I can do?'

'Not tonight, thank you. Tell Althea I've nearly finished, will you?'

Back in the drawing-room Althea was flicking over the pages of a magazine, her face a study in boredom.

'Where's Drewe?' she demanded.

'He asked me to tell you that he'll be out in a moment.'

'And about time too.' Althea threw the magazine viciously onto a table. 'It certainly isn't my idea of hospitality being left alone to amuse myself.'

'I imagine Mr. Chatham thought that

Sara and Ricky would be here.'

'They've gone for a walk, I believe. Oh, they invited me to go with them, but I've no intention of being the unwanted third.' Althea's eyes flickered maliciously over Anna. 'Well, Miss Blakeney, you've dug yourself in here very nicely, haven't you?'

'I don't know what you mean,' began Anna indignantly, but Althea swept in ruthlessly. 'No? Well, it doesn't really matter so long as you realise that your reign's strictly temporary. Drewe and I will be getting married very soon, and he'll have no further need of your services.'

Anna was burning with resentment at Althea's unpleasant attitude, but she'd no intention of entering into a slanging match with her employer's fiancée. Instead she said coolly: 'Naturally I anticipated that.'

'Then we understand each other perfectly.'

'But when I suggested to Mr. Chatham that he wouldn't need me now that Sara was married and Jeremy had settled down again at school he asked me to stay at least until after Christmas.'

Althea frowned, and her lovely eyes became hard and opaque.

'He probably didn't realise that I was willing for the wedding to go ahead. I'll soon put his mind at rest.'

The next moment Drewe Chatham came through the door and she turned to him to say: 'Darling, I've been telling Miss Blakeney that as we're getting married almost immediately I was wondering whether she oughtn't to be looking out for another post. If there's anything I can do to help her find one naturally I will.'

Drewe said calmly: 'The wedding was something I wanted to discuss with you, Althea. I'm afraid that we shall have to postpone it until next Easter.'

'Easter?' Althea's voice rose. 'What's the reason for that?'

Anna felt acutely uncomfortable. They had evidently both forgotten that she was present so she edged her way quickly out of the room, closing the door behind her though not before she'd heard Althea say: 'Drewe, I'm waiting for an explanation,' and thought that it sounded like the beginning of a sizeable row.

She wasn't wrong. Althea's mouth was thinned in fury and she wasn't mollified by Drewe's rejoinder: 'I'm quite ready to give you one, I was merely waiting for Miss Blakeney to leave the room. Now stop looking like an avenging angel, and come and sit down on the sofa.'

Althea sat down and said: 'Well?'

Drewe dropped down beside her, and put his hand over hers.

'I'm sorry, Althea, but while you've been away several important business deals have come up. Now I shall have to travel constantly backwards and forwards to and from the Continent until well after Christmas which was why I suggested we should get married at Easter. Things have been much more difficult for me since my father died. When he was alive he ran the London office but at present there's no one to whom I can delegate the responsibility for that with the result that I have to keep commuting between London and Brussels. I'm training a man who's responding quite well and in a few more months he'll be able to fill in for me at this end of the business, but at the moment I can't leave him to handle things on his own.'

'It all sounds quite ridiculous to me,' said Althea icily. 'Why didn't you mention any of this while we were out today?'

'Because I wanted to forget about the office for a bit and I didn't want to spoil the day for both of us,' answered Drewe frankly. 'Look, my sweet, we haven't seen much of each other all summer. Let's make the best of things and look forward to Easter.'

He slid his arm along the back of the sofa and made to pull her towards him but she wrenched herself away.

'I'm not in the mood for any of that. Drewe, I've made up my mind to be married before Christmas, and I don't see any reason to change my plans.'

'If you prefer it we can be married next weekend by licence but without a honeymoon because I'm flying to Beirut on the Monday. I didn't suggest that alternative since you made it very plain a little while ago that you wouldn't consider what you called a hole and corner wedding.'

'And neither will I,' cried Althea furiously, jumping to her feet. 'If this is your idea of paying me out for refusing earlier to marry you at a moment's notice then I think it's contemptible.'

Now Drewe was on his feet. 'If you think I'm so petty-minded — ' Then his voice softened. 'Althea, I realise you're disappointed and so am I, but it's one of those things. I can't afford to turn away good business. I've Jeremy's future to consider as well as my own.'

'And what about me?' cried Althea. 'That wretched boy comes first with you every time. Drewe, I'm issuing an ultimatum. Either you marry me properly before Christmas or we don't get married at all!'

Drewe stiffened. 'Do you mean that?'

'Yes, I do.' Althea's frustrated pride wouldn't allow her to weaken. She pulled off her diamond and emerald engagement ring and flung it at his feet, then stalked out of the room, storming upstairs to weep tears of baffled rage at having been provoked into breaking her engagement.

Already she was regretting it and deciding that if Drewe apologised in the morning she might agree to take back the ring. She wasn't in love with him but he was the type of man she wanted to marry, and she hadn't met many of those. Her father approved of Drewe, and Althea respected her father's opinion of other men.

So she came down to breakfast prepared to overlook what had been said the night before, providing Drewe was sufficiently contrite, and even willing to postpone the wedding until just after Christmas if it were really necessary, but Drewe didn't give her the chance to be magnanimous. As soon as he saw her he said curtly: 'I take it you won't want to stay on now, Althea, so I'll run you up to town immediately after breakfast,' and then disappeared.

Althea was more furious than ever. Unless she was prepared to crawl, which she'd no intention of doing, the engagement was obviously off for the time being at least. She drank a cup of black coffee, refused anything to eat, and went upstairs to pack.

Anna, having uncomfortable memories of the night before, thought it would be tactful of her not to appear at breakfast so she had her toast and coffee in the kitchen with Mrs. Mabledon. Therefore she had no idea Althea was leaving until Sara sauntered into the kitchen and said: 'Well, that was short and sweet. Althea's gone, and I imagine the engagement must be broken off because she wasn't wearing her ring. I suppose that means Ricky and I won't stand a chance of moving into that flat she hinted about.'

Mrs. Mabledon said blankly: 'Gone? But why?'

Sara shrugged. 'I don't know but obviously Drewe and she must have had a row.'

Anna, feeling guilty, said nothing at all. It wasn't her place to mention last night's quarrel; let Drewe Chatham make whatever explanation he wished.

He didn't return until just before dinner, grim-faced and monosyllabic. Only Ricky's easy flow of conversation saved the meal from becoming an ordeal, and after he and Sara had left Anna began to manufacture an excuse to go up to her room and spend the evening there. However, before she could think of anything her employer said abruptly: 'You've probably guessed that my engagement has been broken off. This will make a difference to my long-term plans but for the present I

shall want you to stay on here. I may close up this house, I'm not sure about that yet, but I'll let you know in plenty of time what I intend to do.'

'Oh,' said Anna in dismay. 'It's such a lovely house.'

'But far too big for a bachelor, particularly one who can only come down at weekends. I'm afraid, Miss Blakeney, that you're sentimental,' he added jeeringly.

'Possibly I am,' retorted Anna with spirit, 'but I fell in love with Heathlands at first sight and I'd hate to see i sold with Jeremy living in a Londo flat.'

'Jeremy will have to get used to a lo of unpleasant things in this life returned his stepbrother grimly.

'That reminds me,' said Anna. 'H half term starts next weekend, and Saturday night he's taking part in production of 'The Mikado'. I thi he's only in the chorus but he see very excited about it. He said in letter that he wished you could see h

too, but realised you would probably be abroad again.'

'As it happens I shall be in England until the following Monday so I ought to take the opportunity to visit the school. We'll go down together to see the show and bring him home.'

'Together?' echoed Anna in surprise.

'Yes, why not? We'll have lunch on the way. What time does 'The Mikado' start?'

'About six. Apparently they're performing it for three nights, but Jeremy only appears on the Saturday which is the last performance.'

There wasn't much time to buy anything new for Saturday so Anna compromised by investing in a new blouse patterned in turquoise, cream and brown to wear with her cinnamon suit and a dashingly brimmed hat in cream felt of which she hoped Jeremy would approve. Drewe Chatham came down on the Friday night but remained shut up in his study so that she saw very little of him until they set off for the

school the next morning.

It was a fine day, and they enjoyed a meal of steak and kidney pie in an hotel on the way. Jeremy was waiting at the school gates with a beaming smile, and greeted them with: 'There's tea and cakes in the library but I can't have any because I have to go and be made up.'

'By the way, Jeremy,' said his stepbrother, 'can we make a quick getaway when the production's over? We've a fair way to drive and I don't want to be too late home.'

'Oh,' said Jeremy disappointedly, 'but the people in the show are going to have a special supper in the library afterwards. Most of them aren't going home until tomorrow and I wondered — '

'Sorry, old boy, but I can't spare the time to come out for you again tomorrow.'

'Couldn't I — ?' began Anna, but Jeremy interposed eagerly: 'You wouldn't need to. Bates Minor's father's coming for him and his brother, and he offered to drop me at home if it would help. Would you like to come and speak to him?'

'I think I'd better.'

Drewe was back in a few minutes, saying: 'That's all fixed. Jeremy will be dropped at Heathlands tomorrow in time for lunch so we don't need to linger tonight. Now I suppose we'd better make an appearance in the library.'

The various housemasters and their wives were present, and a tall woman in black and white came across to them.

'Mr. Chatham, isn't it?' she said, 'and this will be your fiancée. Jeremy told me you were going to be married shortly.'

Anna waited for Drewe Chatham to explain the mistake, but to her amazement he merely smiled and said: 'We're looking forward to 'The Mikado' tonight,' and then cupping her elbow in his hand led her to where the tea and cakes were being dispensed.

6

As he handed her a cup of tea she turned to him in bewilderment and said: 'You left that woman under a false impression. She thinks that we — '

'That we're engaged,' finished Drewe Chatham calmly. 'Don't worry, if necessary I can write to Jeremy and reveal that my engagement's at an end and ask him to tell his housemaster's wife. On the other hand — '

'Yes?' prompted Anna as he allowed the sentence to die away.

'We'll talk on the way home. By the way people are moving it looks as though the performance is due to start very shortly.'

Indeed there was a general exodus towards the small theatre cum concert hall which had been built in the school grounds so Anna and her companion followed the crowd. They had good seats, and Anna thoroughly enjoyed the performance which was very creditable considering all the cast were boys. Jeremy was only in the chorus, but Anna recognised his beaming smile even under a thick coating of make-up and a black wig.

When it was over he came to say goodbye to them, still in his Japanese costume. 'It will soon be Christmas, Anna,' he reminded her anxiously. 'You won't be going away or anything, will you?'

'No,' she assured him. 'We'll decorate a tree and really enjoy ourselves.'

When they were in the car she said: 'I hope I wasn't being reckless in promising Jeremy that I'd still be in the house at Christmas. You won't have sold it by then, will you?'

'No, I shan't have sold it by Chrismas, and whether I sell it at all will depend on you.'

'On me? I don't understand.'

'The reason I didn't tell Jeremy's housemaster's wife that you weren't my fiancée was because I thought it mightn't be necessary. In other words, I'm asking you to marry me.'

'Marry you?' gasped Anna. 'But you don't love me.'

'I have a very high regard for you,' said Drewe Chatham evenly, 'and Jeremy doesn't want to be parted from you. If you and I married and made a home for him it would solve a lot of problems.'

'Yes, but — ' began Anna helplessly. 'I don't think it would work,' she finished.

'Why not?' asked Drewe Chatham reasonably. 'I don't flatter myself that you're in love with me either, but we're sensible people and we've both experienced disappointment. Going into this in a rational fashion I believe we could make a good partnership of it. After all, if you left Heathlands where would you go, and you told me that you liked the place while I know you're fond of Jeremy. For his sake, won't you consider it?'

'But suppose later on you meet someone and fall in love?' queried Anna desperately. 'What then?'

'That's a risk we'd both have to take. As far as I'm concerned I don't think it's very likely, but if we did marry and eventually you found you cared for someone else I wouldn't hold you to our bargain.'

Anna hesitated. She was repelled by the cold-blooded way in which he marshalled the facts, yet she had to admit that there was a lot of sense in what he said. For herself, after the blow of Ricky's marriage she couldn't imagine falling in love with anyone else and it was true that she was very reluctant to leave Jeremy. All the same, was that a strong enough basis for a successful marriage? It wasn't so long since she'd actively disliked Drewe Chatham; could she really contemplate marrying him even if it were for convenience?

'You don't have to decide here and now,' he said. 'Give it consideration and let me know tomorrow how you feel.'

'Thank you,' said Anna. 'I'm tired and I can't think very clearly tonight.'

'Why don't you lean back and doze?' he suggested. 'It will be over an hour before we're home.'

'I'm not as weary as that,' Anna declared, but she was over-confident because as the car sped smoothly along the road she found her eyelids closing. Twice she struggled to sit up straight, but the third time she succumbed and fell fast asleep.

She woke as the car halted outside the front door of Heathlands and blinked dazedly, wondering for a moment where she was. Then a voice in her ear said: 'Wake up, we've arrived,' and she found that she was leaning against her employer's shoulder.

'I'm sorry,' she said confusedly, and scrambled out of the car as quickly as she could. The cold night air banished her sleepiness, and she followed him into the house.

'I don't know about you,' he said, 'but I could do with a hot drink.'

'So could I,' agreed Anna. 'Mrs. Mabledon will have gone to bed but I know my way about the kitchen. I'll make a drink while you're putting the car away. What would you like — tea, coffee or hot chocolate?'

'I haven't had hot chocolate for years but it sounds very inviting. I'll join you in the kitchen in a few moments.'

The kitchen was warm and cosy. Anna put a pan of milk to heat on the electric cooker and brought out yellow flowered mugs and a tin of ginger nuts. Sipping the hot chocolate and watching her employer dip into the biscuit tin she reflected that they might have been any married couple coming home after watching their son perform in a school play, and somehow it was curiously comforting. If she didn't accept Drewe Chatham's proposition she would have to leave Heathlands. She couldn't possibly stay on after she'd refused him but she knew that she didn't want to look for another job. Could she make a success of marriage with him? He would be away a good deal so surely they could manage to live together amicably while he was at home.

It didn't sound very romantic, of course, but perhaps that wasn't a bad thing. She'd given her heart to Ricky, and had suffered a great deal when he rejected her. A marriage of convenience with Drewe Chatham would at least mean that if it came apart her emotions wouldn't be involved. The thought of having to look for a new job or even of returning to the hotel in Cornwall to work didn't appeal to her at all, and she hated the idea of leaving Jeremy.

But suddenly she was too tired to think any more. The hot chocolate had warmed her through and the prospect of bed was inviting. She blinked sleepily, and Drewe Chatham said with a grin: 'You look just like a little owl with ruffled feathers. You'd better go up to bed before you fall asleep in that chair.'

'I think I had,' admitted Anna.

She yawned hugely, and because she was relaxed for once instead of being on her guard with her employer she saw him in a different light. His hair was ruffled too, and losing his high-powered executive air had made him look younger. At that moment it didn't seem quite so impossible to imagine herself married to him, and something of the same impression remained with her the next morning when she knew she'd have to face him at the breakfast table and give him her decision. It wouldn't be fair to keep him in suspense. She must make up her mind one way or the other.

She went down to breakfast, and paused in the hall. A shaft of pale sunlight came through the glass door at the far end which led into the garden, and showed up the leafless beauty of the trees. It occurred to Anna that she'd never seen the garden in the spring and that if she went away now she never would. Absurdly enough that seemed to matter a great deal, and she walked into the dining-room to say before she could stop to consider any longer: 'I'll marry you if you're sure you really want me to.'

Drewe Chatham laid down *The Sunday Times* and rose to his feet.

'I'm quite sure,' he said gravely. 'And you?'

'Yes.'

'Good, that's settled,' he said unemotionally. 'Come and have some breakfast. Bacon and eggs?'

When she refused them and helped herself to toast and honey he picked up the paper again as if nothing out of the ordinary had occurred. Anna felt deflated, then asked herself what she'd expected him to do? Rush round the table and clasp her in his arms? She picked up *The Observer*, and once again the thought struck her that they were behaving like an old married couple so that she had to stifle an hysterical choke of laughter.

After breakfast she went up to make her bed and tidy her room, and when she came down again Drewe was waiting for her.

'Come into the study,' he said. 'We have to make some plans.'

She followed him into the room, and sat down in a comfortably shabby armchair while he propped himself against the end of his desk.

'I propose that we have the wedding at Easter,' he said. 'By then I shall be in a position to take some time off so you must tell me where you'd like to go for a honeymoon.'

'There's just one thing,' pointed out Anna. 'Jeremy will be on holiday from school then and if we're away it will mean making arrangements for him. I'd be willing to be married very quietly and do without a honeymoon.'

'I'm prepared to do my best for Jeremy but I don't propose to sacrifice my whole life to him,' returned Drewe dryly. 'I think he'll survive a fortnight or so here without us. I've no desire for the neighbourhood to think that I've married you in haste to get an unpaid housekeeper.'

'But you were proposing to marry Miss Lymington in haste before you asked me to come here,' Anna couldn't help reminding him.

'That was quite different.'

Why? wondered Anna rebelliously. Because you were marrying her for love?

Aloud she said: 'Let it be Easter then, Mr. Chatham. It doesn't really matter to me.'

'Right, but you'll have to stop calling me 'Mr. Chatham'.'

Anna bit her lip. 'Yes, of course.'

'Well, we can decide about the honeymoon later, but you'd better come up to town with me tomorrow to choose a ring. Then there ought to be an announcement in the papers.'

'Won't it appear rather soon after the breaking off of the other engagement?'

Now it was his turn to look slightly disconcerted.

'Perhaps it will. I imagine Althea's told all her friends that she isn't going to marry me, but as far as I know there hasn't been any official announcement.'

'Then I think it would be better to put that in the papers first and announce our engagement at Christmas,' said Anna firmly.

Drewe looked faintly amused but merely said: 'Just as you wish. I take it then that we aren't officially engaged until Christmas?'

'No, so I shan't mention it to Jeremy when he comes home today.'

Jeremy was dropped in time for lunch and spent four happy days at Heathlands before returning cheerfully to school. Drewe flew to Beirut, and the announcement that the marriage arranged between Mr. Drewe Chatham and Miss Althea Lymington would not now take place was duly inserted in *The Times*.

As soon as she was alone once more Anna began to busy herself with preparations for Christmas, determined that Jeremy should have a good time. She had thought that Sara and Ricky might want to celebrate their first Christmas of married life by themselves, but Sara said frankly that she loathed cooking and was looking forward to spending the holiday at Heathlands.

'Mind you make Sara give you a hand,' said Mrs. Mabledon warningly when Anna was in the kitchen discussing the amount of food they would need. 'You know I'm going to my sister in Margate so if you don't take care you'll find yourself coping with everything on Christmas Day.'

'Oh, it won't be as bad as that, I'm sure,' said Anna optimistically. 'I think I'll order some more tins of those mushrooms cooked in butter. They're a good basis for snacks.'

'And you'll need plenty of those,' prophesied Mrs. Mabledon darkly. 'I don't think Sara cooks a square meal for the pair of them from the time they leave here until they come again, not judging by the way they eat when they are here.'

Anna made out lists and planned menus with a will, and then four days before Christmas she drove to school to pick up Jeremy. He hugged her joyfully as soon as he saw her, and cried: 'Oh, it's so lovely to be going home. I've made a present for Drewe and one for you. I do hope you'll both like them.'

'I'm sure we shall. There's plenty for you to do when we get home. We've the tree and the house to decorate so tomorrow we'll go to the market and see what we can buy.'

'Oh, good.'

The following morning they went to the market in Occambridge, and Jeremy chose a tree which they stowed into the boot of the car. They raided a handsome holly bush in the garden, and then with a plentiful supply of silver frosting and scarlet ribbon they set to work. Because she didn't want him to brood over former Christmases Anna allowed Jeremy to decorate exactly as he chose, only giving him a hand with the awkward spots, and he made a very good job of it.

Drinking hot chocolate before he went to bed he looked round with satisfaction and said: 'Haven't we got a lot of holly? Mrs. Mabledon wouldn't let me hang a kissing ball over the cooker. She said she didn't hold with decorations in the kitchen.'

'Well, sprigs of holly falling in the food wouldn't be exactly pleasant.'

'When will everybody be here?'

'On Christmas Eve. Sara and Ricky are coming in time for dinner, and your stepbrother's flying over in the afternoon.'

'I'm glad that Althea isn't coming and I'm glad that she isn't going to marry Drewe, aren't you?'

This was an awkward question to answer so Anna changed the subject by asking: 'What do you specially want for Christmas?'

'I'd like a transistor radio. We're allowed to have them at school providing we only play them at certain times.'

He'd hinted this before and Anna had passed the word along to Drewe so she was fairly confident that Jeremy would get his wish. She'd bought him some fishing tackle because he'd spoken of going down to the river in the Easter holidays, and she'd thought that if she and Drewe were away on their honeymoon it would be something for the boy to do.

Since he'd been away she'd had several letters from Drewe. They weren't exactly lover-like, but then she could hardly expect that. She'd replied briefly, but she felt curiously shy of meeting him again. It seemed incredible she should be unofficially engaged to marry him. They knew so little about each other really, yet she didn't want to leave Heathlands and Jeremy so if marrying Drewe were the only way to keep them she would go through with it.

By lunchtime on Christmas Eve everything was as nearly ready as it could be, and Jeremy was in a state of wild excitement. The turkey had arrived and Mrs. Mabledon had stuffed it, the pudding needed only a final boiling and the mince pies were in an airtight tin ready to be heated up. Immediately lunch was over Anna drove Mrs. Mabledon to the station to catch her train, and she and Jeremy came back to pile the fire with logs and set out the Christmas cards which arrived by every post. Drewe's plane was due at Heathrow at three o'clock, and allowing a couple of hours for delays and to get through the traffic he should be at Heathlands by five.

But by half past five there was still no sign of him and at six Sara and Ricky arrived, stamping their feet and declaring that it was cold enough for snow.

'I wish it would snow,' exclaimed Jeremy. 'Wouldn't it be super to have a white Christmas?'

'It's even more super to see this fire,' remarked Ricky appreciatively, placing himself squarely in front of it. 'You're looking very charming, Anna. That colour suits you.'

'Thank you,' she said. She was wearing a dress of deep yellow wool trimmed with brown velvet, not new but very becoming. Now for the tenth time she glanced surreptitiously at her watch, wondering why Drewe was so late and hoping that his plane hadn't been delayed by bad weather on the Continent.

Sara said: 'I'm ravenously hungry but I suppose we're waiting to eat until Drewe comes. What time do you expect him?'

'He said he hoped to be here at five, but at holiday times anything can happen.'

All at once there was the sound of a car, and shrieking: 'He's here!' Jeremy rushed to the door. Anna followed, and as Jeremy flung the door open Drewe appeared.

'Hello,' he said. 'A reception committee?'

'We thought you'd never come,' said Jeremy, 'and there's baked ham with madeira sauce for dinner.'

'And we're starving so don't linger,' added Sara.

Anna was conscious of an overwhelming relief at seeing him arrive safe and sound. Until that moment she hadn't realised how anxious she'd been.

'Did you have a bad journey?' she enquired. 'Come and get warm; you must be frozen.'

'I will in a moment,' he answered, and then to her amazement he drew her towards him and kissed her in front of them all.

It took her completely by surprise, and she was so stunned that she made no resistance. It was a swift kiss but there was nothing hesitant about it, in fact it was almost ruthless so that her legs began to tremble, and when Drewe released her she clung to him for a moment for support. She was aware that Sara was staring at them in stupefaction, that Ricky had a little frown between his brows and that

Jeremy's eyes were wide with bewilderment. Drewe was the only person who seemed completely unaffected. He advanced into the drawing-room and said: 'Tell Mrs. Mabledon that she can serve the meal as soon as she likes, will you, Jeremy?'

Jeremy said uncertainly: 'Mrs. Mabledon's gone to stay with her sister. You kissed Anna and you've never done that before.'

'Not in public,' agreed his stepbrother.

'Do you mean there's something between you and Anna, Drewe?' demanded Sara.

'We're engaged to be married. Didn't she tell you?'

'No, she didn't,' answered Sara shortly, and Anna broke in desperately: 'We agreed not to announce it until Christmas.'

'Which it will be in a few hours,' said Drewe blandly. 'This calls for champagne, but since there won't be any on ice I'll put a bottle in the fridge now and we'll drink it after the meal.'

Jeremy cried delightedly: 'Do you mean that you're going to marry Drewe, Anna, and live here for always?'

'I — er — hope so.'

His face lit up. 'Oh, that will be super. It will be almost like it was before.'

He ran to her and flung his arms round her so that she found it difficult to keep back the tears.

Sara said stiffly: 'I hope you'll both be very happy,' and Ricky echoed: 'So do I. You deserve the best, Anna.'

Filled with confusion Anna fled to the kitchen to serve the meal. She felt quite overwhelmed, and wondered what could have possessed Drewe to make such a sudden announcement. The least he could have done was to warn her first.

The champagne was duly drunk after dinner and even Jeremy was allowed a drop, but in spite of it the evening was a sticky one. Ricky could generally be counted on to keep the conversational ball rolling, but tonight he was unusually silent and Sara made no effort to play her part. Things weren't too bad while Jeremy was still up, but when he'd gone protesting to bed the atmosphere was strained. Drewe didn't seem to notice it, interjecting a casual remark into the silence every so often, but Anna longed for the evening to end.

At last Ricky said: 'Come along, Sara, let's go to bed and give the newly-engaged pair a chance to be alone.'

Sara obeyed reluctantly, shooting a smouldering glance at Anna which made the girl's heart sink. Lately the relationship between herself and Sara seemed to have improved; now it was all too obvious that it was back at square one again. She shivered slightly, unwilling to meet Drewe's gaze yet not knowing how to get out of the room without fabricating some clumsy excuse.

He said: 'Come and sit by the fire and get warm. You've looked half frozen all evening.'

'It's nerves, I suppose. You took me

by surprise, announcing the engagement so suddenly.'

'But we agreed to make it public at Christmas.'

'Not so abruptly.'

'Does that kiss rankle?' he enquired softly. 'At the time I thought you co-operated quite well.'

'I — I could hardly slap your face, but you might at least have given me some warning.'

'That I intended to kiss you? But surely it was a natural thing for an engaged couple to do.'

'Of course but — ' As she floundered on Anna suspected that he was laughing at her so she countered with: 'I'm afraid Sara's upset.'

'Which doesn't affect me. She was very emphatic that she had a right to run her own life so she can't deny that privilege to other people.'

Drewe dropped his head back against the chair, and looking at him properly for the first time that evening Anna noticed the deep lines of fatigue round his mouth. She said impulsively: 'You do look tired. Won't you go up to bed now and have an early night? I expect Jeremy will be awake at the crack of dawn tomorrow.'

'I'm sure you're right,' agreed Drewe, pulling himself out of the chair with an obvious effort. 'I've brought his transistor so I'll take it out of my case.'

'He'll be thrilled to have one at last.'

Anna followed him out of the room, and they said good night at the head of the stairs. She had filled a stocking for Jeremy but didn't want to put it in his room until she was quite sure he was asleep so she undressed and slipping a frilled nylon wrap over her nightdress waited another quarter of an hour before creeping along the landing. Jeremy was sound asleep so she placed the fat stocking at the end of his bed and tiptoed out of his room. She was carefully pulling the door to behind her when Drewe came out of his own room, his hair ruffled and a frown of pain between his brows.

'Have you got any aspirin?' he asked. 'I seem to have run out and my head's aching vilely.'

'There's some downstairs,' said Anna, 'but you ought to take it with a hot drink, then you'll probably go off to sleep. It will only take me a few minutes to heat some milk. If you'll go back to bed I'll bring it to you.'

'No need for that, I'll come down with you.'

'It would be much more sensible to go back to bed. You don't want to feel rotten tomorrow.'

To her surprise he obeyed without further protest, and she surmised that his headache must be really bad. She heated the milk and carried it upstairs with the bottle of aspirin to find him sitting up in bed with his eyes closed. Just for a moment she saw a fleeting resemblance to Jeremy, and it gave her an unexpected jolt so that her hand trembled and a little milk slopped onto the tray. She put this hastily down on the bedside table, and as she did so

Drewe's hand shot out and clasped her wrist.

'What's the matter?' he asked. 'Are you afraid I'm going to bite you?'

'Of course not.'

'Then why do you always run away from me?'

'I don't, but it's late now and you ought to lie down and give the tablets a chance to work.'

He dropped her wrist, and said indifferently: 'I suppose you're right. Good night.'

It was what Anna wanted as answering: 'Good night,' she left the room, yet she was conscious of a sense of dissatisfaction.

You're becoming fanciful, she told herself sternly as she went back to her own room, but though she determinedly banished all thought of Drewe and the future from her mind it was a long time before she fell asleep.

As she'd anticipated Jeremy was awake early, and crept into her room to show her the contents of his stocking.

She could have done with at least another hour's sleep but she hadn't the heart to scold him, and tucking him up on her bed with the quilt round him she went quietly down to make a pot of tea which she carried back upstairs. Jeremy thought this was a great treat, and when they'd inspected everything in the stocking she told him to get dressed quietly without rousing the house and come down to the kitchen. Since she was up she decided she might as well carry on with some jobs so by eight-thirty when she heard someone else stirring she had the preparations for breakfast well under way and the turkey all ready in the oven.

It was Ricky who appeared, and Anna asked him if Sara would like breakfast in bed.

'I imagine she would since she only grunted when I got up,' he answered, 'but not if it's too much trouble.'

'It isn't if you'll take her up a tray. Jeremy, would you run up to see if Drewe would also prefer his breakfast in bed. He had a bad headache last night.'

'All right,' said Jeremy obligingly.

Ricky propped himself up by the cooker as Anna slid bacon under the grill.

'It was a shock last night to discover you were going to marry Drewe,' he said. 'I wouldn't have thought that he was your type.'

'Wouldn't you?'

'You're not doing it just to — well, just to give yourself a home, are you, Anna?'

'Why shouldn't I?' Anna flipped the bacon over. 'I have to consider the future.'

'Yes, but Drewe of all people. You told me that you didn't like him.'

'That was — '

Anna stopped short as a voice behind her said: 'Thank you for the offer of breakfast in bed, but I much prefer to get up for it.'

'Oh.' Anna whirled round; wondering how much Drewe had heard. 'Are you feeling better this morning?'

'A great deal better,' he assured her, but he still looked pale and she noticed that although he drank two cups of coffee he ate very little. After breakfast Jeremy opened his main presents and was delighted with the transistor and the fishing tackle. Ricky and Sara had given him a camera which he was wild to try out so after breakfast the three males went for a walk, leaving Anna to carry on with the preparations for lunch.

Sara drifted down about eleven and offered to set the table so Anna left her to it. The men came back at twelve and at a quarter to one everything was ready to be dished up. The bird was plump and golden brown while the pudding was rich and spicy so that the meal was voted a great success. After the table was cleared and the dirty dishes loaded into the dish washer everyone lay back lazily to drink coffee.

Sara looked expectantly at her husband.

'Go on,' she said. 'Now's as good a time as any.'

'Not yet,' answered Ricky. 'We're all too full of food.'

'You're only making excuses. Tell Drewe now,' she insisted.

'Tell me what?' enquired Drewe.

'Oh, very well,' said Ricky resignedly. 'The fact is, Drewe, that I'm not happy in my present job. I've tried to pull my weight but it simply isn't working out so the best thing is for me to make a change.'

'And what do you propose to do?'

'Well, Hilary, the cousin I worked with when I first came to London, wants me to go back into interior decorating with her and this time if I can put up some capital she's willing to make me a partner. That would make all the difference, of course. I shouldn't be a general dogsbody as I was before, and I think I could make a success of it.'

'So do I,' broke in Sara. 'You've definitely got a flair for line and colour,

Hilary admits that.'

'And where do I come into this? Do you want me to let you go without notice?'

'Rather more than that, I'm afraid.'

'We want you to lend Ricky the money to go into partnership,' interrupted Sara impetuously. 'You can easily afford it, Drewe, and he'll pay you back as soon as he can.'

'How much would you need to buy yourself this partnership?' asked Drewe.

'Hilary wants £5,000.'

Drewe's eyebrows rose. 'Does she indeed?'

'It might sound a lot of money but it isn't a fortune these days,' said Sara impatiently. 'Will you lend it to us, Drewe?'

'Not until I've investigated the business, seen a balance sheet and a set of audited accounts,' replied Drewe uncompromisingly, and Sara exploded.

'Oh, you're always so damned cautious. With you it's wait every time. Wait for what? Until we're so old and decrepit that we haven't the strength to launch out into anything? It's now that we want things and not in some dim and distant future.'

'You won't have anything either now or in the future if you rush into wild schemes without due consideration,' pointed out Drewe. He turned to Ricky. 'If your cousin's a good business woman she'll realise that no one's going to invest money in a partnership without making enquiries first.'

Ricky couldn't conceal his disappointment. 'Hilary's a good business woman but she also has a quick temper. She thought she was doing me a favour offering me a partnership and I don't think she'll take very kindly to being asked for audited accounts and a balance sheet when it's all in the family, so to speak.'

'That kind of attitude's been responsible for far more losses than gains,' retorted Drewe, unmoved, and Sara sprang to her feet.

'Keep your money,' she flung at him.

'I'll sell the shares you transferred to me and hand over the proceeds to Ricky.'

Drewe's mouth firmed in exasperation. 'Don't be a little fool. The market's depressed at the moment and you won't get anything like the true value of those shares.'

'What does that matter? At least I'll be able to acquire some money without having to crawl to you for it.'

Drewe went very white, and Anna could see that he was only holding his temper in leash by a tremendous effort.

'I don't intend to argue any further with you, Sara,' he said grimly. 'I'll lend you the money if the state of this business warrants it and not unless,' and he got up and walked out of the room.

'Good riddance,' said Sara viciously. 'Come on, Ricky, let's go out and breathe some fresh air,' and with an apologetic look at Anna Ricky followed her.

Anna sighed. It seemed as if Sara and

her stepbrother would always be at loggerheads, and she didn't relish the role of buffer state. Jeremy glanced up from the jigsaw puzzle he was doing and said kindly: 'Never mind, Anna, Sara always argues a lot, but don't take any notice of her.'

'That's rather difficult,' said Anna ruefully. 'How are you progressing with that jigsaw?'

'There are rather a lot of blue pieces which could be either the sky or the sea, but I've nearly completed the ship. Will there be crumpets for tea and Christmas cake?'

'You couldn't possibly manage anything after that enormous lunch, could you?'

Jeremy grinned at her. 'I can always manage Christmas cake.'

Sara and Ricky returned in time for tea at which Drewe also put in an appearance, and to Anna's relief the argument wasn't renewed. In the evening they watched television and Boxing Day passed off uneventfully too so that by the time Sara and Ricky were ready to return to London Anna was hoping that they were willing to come to terms with Drewe over the loan. This hope was dashed, however, when she was in the bedroom helping Sara to finish her packing.

'I wish you joy of marrying Drewe,' said Sara emphatically as she peered under the bed for her slippers and crammed them into her case. 'You'll have to go down on your knees to him every time you want anything new.'

'That's not fair,' protested Anna. 'It's only common sense, Sara, for him to make some enquiries before lending Ricky all that money.'

'Ricky's perfectly capable of using his own judgement,' snapped Sara. 'After all, he worked in the business so he should know whether or not it was well run. No, it's just that Drewe likes to have people under his thumb. He revels in the fact that the money Daddy left is tied up in the business, and since he is the trustee for my share and Jeremy's until we reach twenty-one we can only have what he doles out. But he can't stop me selling those shares and I shall do that just as soon as I can.'

'Please, Sara, think it over and don't do anything you may regret later. Why not let Drewe make his investigation? If everything's in order I'm sure you'll find him generous.'

'No,' said Sara obstinately. 'I'm not knuckling under to him any longer,' and she closed the locks of her case with a vicious snap.

Plainly it was no use arguing further with her, but Anna hoped that Ricky would prove more amenable and resolved to have a word with him before he left. But in this she was foiled. Ricky was having trouble with the car, and by the time he'd traced the fault to the plugs and rectified it he was anxious to be on his way. With a brief farewell he and Sara departed without Anna having had an opportunity to ask him to persuade his wife to see reason.

When Drewe drove away to London

the next morning leaving Anna alone with Jeremy, she pondered on how to get in touch with Ricky. She didn't want to ring him at the office because of the difficulty he would have in talking privately yet she must speak to him soon in case Sara should do anything precipitate. Perhaps it was foolish of her to worry over the relationship between Drewe and Sara or care whether or not there was a breach between them, but the fact remained that she wanted them to be good friends and she knew that if Sara sold those shares Drewe would find it hard to forgive her. The easiest way to clinch the matter would be to go up to London to see Ricky, but there was Jeremy to consider.

Then Alastair's mother rang up to ask if they could take Jeremy out the next day, and the problem was solved. Anna decided to ring Ricky at the office and ask him to have lunch with her.

'That is if you're not meeting Sara,' she said. 'I must talk to you, and this is probably the only opportunity I'll have in the near future.'

'All right,' he said. 'Where shall we meet?'

'I'll wait for you by the Underground station at the end of the street.'

'I'll be there at one.'

As soon as Jeremy had been picked up the next morning Anna set off herself, and after doing a little shopping she took up her position outside the Underground station to wait for Ricky. She had been waiting only a few minutes when she saw him coming towards her.

'I'm sorry not to be here on the dot,' he apologised, 'but I was held up by a telephone call just as I was about to leave the office.'

'It doesn't matter, I haven't been waiting long,' Anna told him. 'Ricky, I know I've no right to interfere in your affairs but I felt I had to talk to you.'

'Then let's go and eat. There's a restaurant not far from here which I sometimes use because it's fairly quiet and serves reasonably good food.'

He put his hand under her elbow to guide her across the road as a taxi shot past, neither of them sparing a glance for its occupant. It happened to be Althea, and when she saw them she immediately ordered the driver to pull up.

'I've changed my mind,' she said. 'I'll get out here,' and she paid him off quickly, trying to keep Anna and Ricky in sight.

In this she was lucky. They were held up by traffic, and she managed to cross the road in time to see them disappear into a restaurant. She followed them and sauntered into the restaurant herself, looking about her until she saw them sitting together at a table and talking earnestly. Then she coolly walked out again, hailing another taxi with a malicious smile curving her lips.

7

Anna arrived home in the late afternoon, wondering if she'd achieved anything. When she'd asked Ricky to try to persuade Sara not to act hastily but to wait a little while until Drewe had investigated the business he was evasive, and she almost wished she'd left matters as they were.

If she'd known that Althea had seen her and Ricky together she would certainly have regretted meeting him because the other girl lost no time in making use of her discovery. She rang up Sara and said: 'About that flat. I haven't forgotten but I've no news to report as yet. The owner's still away.'

'I thought perhaps you wouldn't be bothering now,' said Sara frankly.

'You mean because I'm no longer engaged to Drewe?' Althea managed quite a convincing laugh. 'My dear, I hope I'm not as petty-minded as that. Did you go down to Heathlands for Christmas?'

'Yes, but I ended up having a row with Drewe as usual. He really is too domineering for words. Anna Blakeney may think she's done a good thing for herself, but she'll pay for it in more ways than one. I wouldn't marry Drewe if he were hung with gold.'

'Marry?' Althea's voice sharpened. 'What do you mean?'

'Oh, lord.' Sara sounded guilty. 'I didn't mean to say anything about that but you'd have found out before long, anyway. Drewe and Anna are going to be married.'

'Are they indeed?' Althea was seething. She'd never liked Anna, and her object in ringing Sara was to set her against the girl in the hope of winkling her out of Heathlands. Now she was doubly anxious to do Anna some harm. 'That's quick work, isn't it? Off with the old and on with the new with a vengeance.'

'Well, Drewe needed someone to look after Jeremy and I imagine that's why he proposed to Anna.'

'And she decided to marry a man who could give her a comfortable home while at the same time having fun with Ricky on the side.'

Now it was Sara's turn to ask: 'What do you mean?'

'They were lunching together in town today.'

'Are you sure?'

'I saw them myself. I was about to get out of a taxi when I noticed them crossing the road together and watched them go into a restaurant. I'm not blaming Ricky half as much as her. I'll swear she was the one who suggested the meeting, and you ought to be on your guard, Sara, before this affair goes any further.'

'Yes,' said Sara slowly. 'Thank you, Althea, for letting me know.'

'And if I hear anything about the flat I'll be in touch. Goodbye.'

Ricky was late home that evening,

and Sara began to imagine all kinds of things so that by the time he did arrive she'd worked herself up into a fury. She taxed him immediately with meeting Anna and he admitted that Anna had been the one to ring him, adding unwisely that she'd asked him to use his influence with Sara to persuade her to be patient and wait until Drewe had investigated Hilary's business before taking any action. This incensed his wife even more.

'What business of hers is it how I use my money? She has no right to interfere in my affairs, and I shall go down to Heathlands and tell her so!'

Ricky shrugged, having already learnt the futility of trying to turn Sara from any course of action upon which she was determined.

'Why do that? Now that she's going to marry Drewe it seems a pity to stir up fresh trouble.'

'Because this could be just the beginning. I don't believe she's ever forgiven me for annexing you, and she'd have no scruples in trying to get you back.'

'What rubbish. She isn't that kind of girl at all.'

Ricky's defence of Anna only sharpened Sara's apprehensions, and because she was uneasy her instinct was to strike at her enemy. Without giving herself time to reflect she bounced down to Heathlands the next day, and discovering that Drewe was at home confronted Anna in his presence.

'How dare you set out to meet Ricky behind my back,' Sara flamed. 'It was a filthy trick, and if it hadn't been for someone seeing you together I don't suppose I should have known anything about it.'

'You've jumped to the wrong conclusion,' protested Anna unhappily, aware that the only explanation she could give wasn't going to sound convincing. 'I only wanted to help.'

From the background Drewe said: 'Calm down, Sara, and let's get to the bottom of this. Who saw what?'

'Someone — oh well, if you must know it was Althea — saw Anna and Ricky lunching together in town yesterday. When I tackled Ricky about it he said it was true, but that Anna rang him and asked him to lunch with her.'

'Yes, I did,' Anna confirmed, 'but did he tell you why?'

'Some ridiculous excuse about wanting him to persuade me not to act hastily over this question of a partnership,' said Sara scornfully, 'but I didn't believe that for a moment.'

'Why not?' queried Drewe coolly.

'Because Anna and I have never hit it off so why should she be concerned over a breach between you and me? She'd be glad of anything which drove a wedge between us and stopped me from coming to the house.'

'That isn't true,' cried Anna indignantly. 'I tried to talk to you before you left but you wouldn't listen to me so I approached Ricky instead.'

'You don't need to plead with Ricky or with me. I won't have you interfering in my affairs so keep out of them.'

Sara whirled round, and Drewe said in chilly tones: 'There's no need for dramatics. If you've said all you want to say, Sara, then you'd better go back to London. I can't imagine why you came down here in the first place or what you expected to gain by it.'

'I was determined to warn Anna off my husband and also to open your eyes. If you're still determined to go through with this marriage then I wish you joy of it.'

If Drewe's voice had been cold before it was positively glacial now. 'I'll remind you of what you just said to Anna. I won't have you interfering in my affairs so keep out of them.'

Sara made an infuriated sound and shot through the door. They heard the car start up, and when it had roared off Anna said shakily: 'I never imagined I'd cause all this trouble or I wouldn't have dreamed of ringing Ricky.'

'Wouldn't you?'

She stared at him. 'Do you mean you

don't believe the explanation I gave?'

'Did you expect me to?'

'But — ' Suddenly her temper exploded. 'If you think I lied then there's not much point in our getting married, is there? It would be better for us to call the whole thing off and for me to go away.'

'Now you're becoming as dramatic as Sara and I've no intention of calling the whole thing off. Could you visualise what that would do to Jeremy? He's beginning to regain his self-confidence; do you want to plunge him into uncertainty again?'

'No, of course not.' Anna made an effort to steady herself, adding: 'Only if — ' but Drewe had turned away and she was talking to herself.

It was just as well, she reflected, that he was returning to Brussels the next day. She felt so mixed up about everything that she needed a period for reflection. Had Drewe believed her or not? She simply couldn't tell which wasn't a very good augury for their marriage. She could see now that it would have been wiser to let matters take their course since she'd only succeeded in worsening the relationship between Sara and herself, but she resented being made to feel like a criminal.

Fortunately Jeremy kept her from brooding over events, and by the time he returned to school she'd settled down to live for the moment and let the future take care of itself. Sara and Ricky had come down for Jeremy's last weekend, and for his sake an uneasy truce prevailed in the house. Anna learned that Ricky was working out his notice at Chatham Exports and that he would soon be starting with Hilary again. Evidently Sara was using her money to pay for the partnership, but in spite of this she didn't appear very happy and it was a relief when they went back to London.

A month went by and Anna occupied herself in rearranging some of the furniture and starting an early spring clean. Drewe wrote several times, brisk, rather impersonal letters to which Anna dutifully replied. She felt as if she were poised on the edge of a precipice, uncertain whether to draw back or to jump, and she avoided thinking about Drewe's return and the decision she must come to then.

One Friday afternoon when there was a touch of mildness in the air and it seemed as though spring couldn't be far away Anna arrived back from a walk and was taking off her coat when the bell rang. She dropped the coat onto a chair and to her surprise opened the door to Ricky.

He said: 'Hello, Anna. I was visiting a client in the neighbourhood, and thought I'd call on you.'

'Come in,' invited Anna. 'I was about to make some tea so you can join me in a cup.'

'Thanks.'

Ricky walked into the study, and Anna said: 'Mrs. Mabledon lit the fire in here because Drewe's expected home tonight. Sit down while I make the tea.'

Once upon a time a *tête à tête* with Ricky would have filled her with joy, but now she discovered that she was sorry he'd called. She'd been looking forward to tea by the fire with a book, but now she would have to make conversation instead.

When she returned with the tea trolley she said: 'Is the job coming up to expectation this time?'

'Yes,' answered Ricky, taking a piece of toasted tea-cake. 'Being in partnership with Hilary is a very different thing from trailing behind her like a lackey but life is difficult in other directions. Sara's become abnormally possessive. She'll hardly let me out of her sight.'

'In view of what happened recently I was rather surprised to see you today,' observed Anna dryly. 'Does Sara know you're visiting me?'

'No, she doesn't, but I can't allow her to choose my friends for me. Since you and I lunched together I've had to account for all my movements and undergo an inquisition every night as to what I've been doing during the day. You know, Anna, I'm beginning to think that I made a mistake in marrying her.'

'It's rather late to decide that and you owe her a great deal — the cost of the partnership, for instance.'

'But there are limits to gratitude, and she doesn't own me body and soul.'

'No, but you knew she was temperamental and obstinate when you married her. You always have to pay for what you want in this life.'

'You're not very sympathetic,' said Ricky in hurt astonishment. 'You've changed, Anna.'

Anna was aware of it too. She'd never imagined herself speaking like that to Ricky, and it amazed her to realise that she felt something akin to contempt for him. It was as if she were seeing him clearly for the first time in her life — still handsome and attractive but weak and full of self-pity. How could she ever have believed she was in love with him? It occurred to her that however shabbily life treated Drewe he wouldn't whine but would set himself to overcome his difficulties.

She said: 'Sara's wilful and intolerant but she's very young, Ricky, and she's lost both her parents. You'll have to be patient with her; you can't abandon a marriage which has hardly begun.'

'It's easy to talk,' he began sulkily, 'but you don't understand. I'm working hard and when I get home I want some peace and comfort not a rapid fire of questions and an indifferent meal. If Sara had taken a cookery course instead of a modelling course she'd have been much better equipped for married life.' He bit into a slice of chocolate cake. 'This is the first decent food I've had today. Sara had forgotten to buy any bacon for breakfast, the milk had gone sour, and I only had time to snatch a sandwich for lunch.'

'I'll go and make some fresh tea,' said Anna, and picked up the teapot. As she went through the door the telephone rang, and stretching out his arm Ricky said: 'I'll answer it.'

With a flash of premonition Anna cried: 'No, don't,' but it was too late. Even as he said: 'Hello,' his face changed and in a second he dropped the receiver back on its rest.

'Oh lord,' he groaned, 'that was Sara.'

'Did she recognise your voice?'

'Yes. She said: 'Ricky, what are you doing there?' and then I cut her off.'

'Oh, dear.' Anna put down the teapot, her eyes troubled. 'You know, Ricky, it was idiotic of you to come down here at all, and even more stupid of me to let you in. You'll have to get home as quickly as you can and convince Sara that you only called for a cup of tea.'

'But how?'

'That's your problem,' replied Anna crisply, 'and it won't be solved by your lingering here. Besides, though I'm not expecting Drewe until later on it's possible that he might arrive early, and I don't want him to find you here. And,

Ricky, please don't call again unless Sara is with you.'

'Don't worry, I won't,' vowed Ricky bitterly. 'We've known each other a long time, Anna, and I'd never have believed you could be so hard. I always felt I could turn to you whatever happened.'

'You have a wife to rely on now, and I have a fiancé. We can't go back, Ricky, and I don't even want to.'

With an aggrieved look Ricky walked to the door, and Anna said goodbye to him with relief. Why did fate ordain that Sara should ring this particular afternoon? She would never believe now that Anna and Ricky weren't having an affair, and if she came storming down to Heathlands again Anna would find it more than difficult to convince Drewe that she was completely innocent. Suddenly it mattered a great deal that he shouldn't misjudge her. There was only one thing for it. She would have to tell him everything herself before Sara could accuse her.

So it was with a feeling of sick apprehension that Anna heard his car pull up outside the house about six o'clock. She sprang to her feet when she heard his key in the lock and went to meet him, then when she saw him she momentarily forgot her anxiety in concern.

'You look worn out,' she said. 'Come and sit by the fire and I'll get you a drink. Have you had a difficult time in Brussels?'

'Pretty gruelling,' he admitted. 'Some rather important negotiations went sour on me, and it's taken every ounce of tact and persuasion I could muster to smooth things over.'

'And have you succeeded?'

'I hope so.'

He lay back in his chair, sipping the whisky and soda Anna had mixed for him, and said: 'It's good to be home.'

A warm glow spread over her. If she could do nothing more for him she could at least make him comfortable and give him peace in his leisure moments.

'I've great plans for the garden next spring,' she said. 'I thought we might plant daffodils and narcissi under those trees behind the swimming pool, and a wide drift of grape hyacinths at the edge of the rose border.'

'Whatever you like,' he agreed. 'If you can take an interest in the garden so much the better, otherwise it might be lonely for you when Jeremy's at school and I'm away. What did you do with yourself today?'

She knew he was only trying to take a polite interest in her doings, but he'd never asked that question before and it couldn't have come at a worse time. She had to make a lightning decision whether to answer noncommittally and tell him about Ricky later or whether to come out with it now. She didn't want to spoil his relaxed mood but she felt it was important she should be open with him, that there was nothing he would loathe more than deceit and evasion.

So as casually as she could she said: 'Well, I had an unexpected visitor this afternoon. Ricky was in the neighbourhood visiting a client so he called and I gave him tea.'

She was aware that Drewe's eyes were fixed steadily on her face but she had to continue. Should she mention what they'd talked about, tell him that Ricky's marriage wasn't running smoothly? No, better not, she decided in a flash. If it all blew over as she hoped it would Sara wouldn't thank her husband for revealing their differences.

With only a momentary hesitation Anna went on: 'We chatted about this and that, and he told me he's enjoying his new job. Unfortunately just as I was leaving the room to make some fresh tea the telephone rang and he answered it, only to find that it was Sara calling. Naturally she recognised his voice and he banged down the receiver. It was all quite harmless but — '

'Of course Sara will find it difficult to believe that,' finished Drewe expressionlessly.

'Yes.'

He put down his glass and stood up.

'Would you have told me about Ricky's visit if it hadn't been for that telephone call?'

Anna said slowly as if the words were dragged out of her: 'No, I don't think I would. Ricky's visit was quite unexpected and I didn't really want to see him because I'd been for a walk and I was tired, but I'm aware that it's not a very convincing tale.'

'Exactly,' retorted Drewe, and walked out of the room.

Anna felt extraordinarily desolate. She hadn't allowed herself to assume that Drewe would accept her explanation without question but she realised now that at the back of her mind there'd been the faint hope that he would. Instead the gulf between them had widened, and she didn't know how to bridge it.

At round about the same time Ricky was enduring the full gamut of Sara's wrath. He'd put off going back to the flat as long as he could, and when he did arrive there cold and hunger had blunted some of the guilt he felt. Consequently his determination to apologise right away in the hope of averting a scene dwindled when he found himself faced with a flushed, tear-stained wife, a disorderly flat and no sign whatever of a meal.

As soon as she saw him Sara jumped to her feet.

'So you've condescended to come home at last,' she raged. 'You needn't have bothered.'

'Look, Sara,' he began placatingly, 'I can explain how I came to be at Heathlands when you rang up this afternoon. I was in the neighbourhood and I popped in to have a word with Anna who told me that she was expecting Drewe home this evening.'

'To warn you not to stay too long, I suppose.'

'Nothing of the sort. Let's have something to eat, and talk properly.'

'If you want a meal you'll have to get

it yourself. Not that there's anything in. I'd intended to go shopping this afternoon, but as you can imagine I'd other things on my mind. Go back to Heathlands and let Anna feed you!'

She flung herself into a chair and Ricky went to investigate the contents of the fridge. Sara had spoken the truth. It was empty apart from a few limp lettuce leaves and half a tub of yoghurt while the bread bin yielded nothing but a stale crust.

Now Ricky's anger rose and overflowed at the sight of the malicious smile on his wife's face when he came back into the sitting-room.

'Damn it, Sara,' he began furiously, 'you're the world's worst housekeeper and it can't take much effort to run a flat the size of this one. Heaven knows how you'll cope with modelling engagements if they do turn up.'

'If you're not satisfied go back to your girl-friend,' Sara jeered. 'I'm sure you wish you'd married her instead of me, only of course she hadn't any money, had she?'

That was the final insult, none the less penetrating because of the stab of truth in it. Ricky picked up his coat, and pulling it on made for the door.

'This is the end. I'm going and I shan't come back!'

Sara realised that she'd gone too far.

'You're cruel,' she wailed. 'I didn't mean what I said; I'm not feeling well. I haven't felt well all week. I think I'm going to have a baby.'

But it was too late. If Ricky heard her last words then he didn't heed them but slammed the door resoundingly behind him. Sara subsided into tears of fright and misery, and when she was exhausted with crying she dragged herself to the telephone and dialled a number.

To the voice which answered she said: 'Is that you, Althea? It's Sara. I'm all alone. Ricky's gone and I feel ill. Please help me.'

'Don't worry,' replied Althea immediately. 'I'll be round in the shortest possible time.'

She was as good as her word. Sara dragged herself to the door to open it and Althea walked in, saying briskly: 'Now what's the matter and where's Ricky?'

'Gone,' moaned Sara. 'I can't stay here alone. Oh, what am I going to do?'

'Isn't Ricky coming back? Tell me exactly what's happened.'

The tale came tumbling out, and then Sara broke down again. 'Stay with me, Althea. Don't leave me.'

'You ought to go down to Heathlands. After all, it's your home.'

'But Drewe will be there tonight, Ricky said so, and he won't want me butting in.'

A gleam came into Althea's eye. 'Nonsense, it's much the best place for you and Drewe will never refuse to put you up. Get your coat on and I'll collect some things together for you and drive you down.'

Sara was inclined to protest, but Althea didn't give her the chance to say much. She thrust toilet things and night-clothes into a weekend bag and had the girl in the car before Sara was really aware of what she was doing. Sara slumped in her seat, more dazed than hysterical now, and Althea with triumph started the car.

Dinner was over and Drewe and Anna were having coffee in the drawing-room when the bell rang. It had been a silent meal and now there was tension in the air so that Anna wished he would say something, anything, to relieve the tautness of her nerves. The sound of the bell made her start visibly, and Drewe said sharply: 'Are you expecting anyone?'

She shook her head, saying: 'No,' as they heard Mrs. Mabledon go to the door. Then a familiar voice enquired: 'Is Mr. Drewe in, Mrs. Mabledon?' and the next moment Althea was in the room.

'Hello, Drewe,' she greeted him casually. 'Sorry to barge in on you like this but I've brought Sara down. She rang me up in an hysterical condition, and since I couldn't leave her alone in the flat I thought this was the best place for her.'

Mrs. Mabledon supported Sara into the room and the girl sank into a chair, her coat pulled on over the sweater and trousers she was wearing, her face swollen with weeping.

'I was in rather a quandary,' said Althea ruefully. 'Apparently Ricky walked out on her after a quarrel. Sara mentioned something about Anna and that Ricky had been here today. I couldn't grasp all she said.'

She looked apologetically at Drewe, and his face hardened.

'I know all about that. Sara, pull yourself together and tell me what's happened.'

Sara lay back in the chair with her eyes closed.

'Ricky's gone,' she whimpered.

'I wondered if we ought to call a doctor,' said Althea. 'Sara thinks that she's going to have a baby and complained of feeling ill.'

'Then we'll certainly have the doctor,'

said Drewe. 'Anna, will you ring him? In the meantime the best place for Sara is bed.'

'The spare room bed's aired,' broke in Mrs. Mabledon who had been hovering in the background. 'I'll just put the sheets on it.'

'You and I can get her upstairs between us, Drewe,' declared Althea. 'Come along, Sara.'

Anna contacted the doctor, and then went into the kitchen where Mrs. Mabledon was whisking up an egg-nog.

'This is a fine to-do,' commented the housekeeper. 'If Sara thinks she's going to have a baby and didn't feel well then Miss Lymington should have put her to bed in the flat and not brought her on a car journey. Suppose she'd had a miscarriage on the way?'

'I thought of that,' responded Anna, 'but I suppose with Ricky gone the situation was rather awkward.'

'Miss Lymington wanted an excuse to come down here herself,' retorted Mrs. Mabledon. 'It's my belief she regrets ever having broken off her engagement, but it's too late now.'

But was it? wondered Anna. Did Drewe also regret having proposed to her, Anna, on the rebound, and if so what ought she to do about it? She was still debating this when the doctor arrived and she showed him up to the spare room where Sara was now in bed.

'Let's have a look at you,' he said breezily, and Drewe followed Anna out of the room. He was frowning, and her heart sank. He'd been so tired when he arrived home; why couldn't they have had a peaceful weekend to give him a chance to relax?

The doctor soon came downstairs again. 'Nothing much wrong there,' he pronounced, 'but I should say she's almost certainly pregnant and she ought to take things easily for a while. Where's her husband?'

'That's what I'm trying to find out,' said Drewe grimly. 'Apparently they had a quarrel when he arrived home this evening, and he flung out.'

'He's probably back all ready to make it up by now, and the best thing too.'

'And if he isn't?'

'Then she mustn't be allowed to brood. Keep her cheerful, and don't allow her to imagine herself an invalid. I'll drop in again tomorrow.'

As Drewe was showing him to the door Althea came down the stairs.

'I'm sorry for letting you in for this, Drewe,' she apologised, 'but I didn't really know what to do for the best.'

'You did the right thing by bringing Sara here. I'm glad you were at hand.'

'She was completely uncontrolled and almost incoherent. I couldn't make out why Ricky had stormed out of the flat except that it was because he had visited Anna here this afternoon and Sara found out when she rang up and he answered the telephone.'

Anna said: 'Ricky was visiting a client near here so he called in for a cup of tea. When the telephone rang he was near it so he answered it.'

'Oh, I see,' murmured Althea. 'Sara seemed to think there was much more behind it than that, but then pregnant women do get queer fancies, don't they? From what she said I got the impression that you and Ricky had been constantly meeting on the sly. Do you mind if I go and tidy myself? When Sara rang she sounded so distraught that I dashed out without even glancing in the mirror.'

When she'd gone Anna turned to Drewe. 'You don't need to worry about Sara. I'll look after her.'

She thought he regarded her strangely. 'Will you? Well, perhaps for a little while until I can make other arrangements.'

'You're talking as if Ricky had gone for ever,' exclaimed Anna. 'I think that the doctor's right and he's probably back at the flat now wondering where Sara is.'

'In that case he'd surely ring up here since Althea left a note explaining where Sara had gone.'

'Oh — yes.'

Althea appeared, bandbox fresh, and smiled up at Drewe.

'I'd love a drink,' she confided. 'All this has been rather a strain.'

'I'm sorry, Althea, I ought to have offered you one before this. Come and sit down. Have you had any dinner?'

'As a matter of fact, I haven't. I was about to sit down to it when Sara rang.'

'Then you must have something.'

'I'll cut some sandwiches,' said Anna quickly.

'Thanks.' Drewe looked down at Althea and she put her hand on his arm.

'Tell me all you've been doing, Drewe. How are things in the business?'

A wave of jealousy swept over Anna so that she was appalled by the strength of her reaction to Althea's monopolisation of Drewe. It could only mean one thing, and she acknowledged now that she'd been wilfully deluding herself for some time. She'd refused to face the fact that she was in love with him, that her early antipathy towards him had vanished completely and that she wanted nothing so much as to marry him and make a home for him.

But what did he feel for her? It wasn't so very long since he'd been engaged to Althea; would he ever be able to forget her? From the way they were talking together Anna thought it was doubtful, and as she went to the kitchen her mind was in a turmoil. Mrs. Mabledon suggested an omelet instead of the sandwiches, and Anna offered to wait until it was ready. She longed for Althea to leave, and willed her to eat the omelet as quickly as possible and start back for London.

Unfortunately Althea showed no sign of departing. She ate the omelet, praising it extravagantly, and then went on chatting to Drewe, giving him the latest news of one mutual friend after another and obviously entertaining him because he laughed a lot. Cleverly she kept Anna out of the conversation so that the girl felt herself the unwanted third.

She glanced at the clock, judging that Althea must leave soon, and then to her relief heard the other girl say: 'Well, I suppose I ought to be on my way if I'm to get back at a reasonable hour. Not that there'll be anyone to greet me apart from the housekeeper. Daddy's away so I have to amuse myself, and town's so boring at the weekends with all one's friends in the country. It's so much pleasanter here that I'm quite reluctant to tear myself away.'

'Then why not stay until Sunday?' suggested Drewe.

'But if Sara's here you won't want to be bothered with an extra visitor.'

'There's Jeremy's room and one more to meals won't make any difference, will it, Anna?'

'No, of course not,' stammered Anna, trying to conceal her dismay. 'I'll just have a word with Mrs. Mabledon.'

She helped the housekeeper to get Jeremy's room ready for the unexpected guest, sick fear creeping over her. This invitation underlined the fact that

Drewe didn't object to Althea's company and she made no secret of the fact that she still found him attractive. Mrs. Mabledon made no comment, but Anna remembered what she'd said about Althea regretting her broken engagement and knew it was true.

If only she had an excuse to slip away for a few days and leave him to make up his mind which of them he preferred, but she'd promised to look after Sara. Anna realised that she would have to stay on until the other girl was better, but it was going to be torture for her to watch Drewe and Althea together this weekend.

When she returned to the drawing-room Althea was saying: 'Fortunately I put a few things in a zipper bag because I wasn't sure quite how long I'd have to stay with Sara so I won't need to borrow a toothbrush. I'll telephone the housekeeper to let her know where I am, and that will be that.'

She didn't trouble to disguise her satisfaction at the success of her manoeuvre, but Drewe gave no sign of having issued the invitation against his will. In her despair Anna almost asked him point-blank if he wanted to break off this second engagement, but before she could bring the words out Althea was back in the room, declaring gaily: 'Well, that's all fixed up. Have you any new recordings, Drewe? If so I'd love to hear them.'

At any other time Anna would have revelled in the music but now it brought back tormenting memories of that evening she and Drewe had spent together.

Althea said laughingly: 'I do believe Anna's half asleep, but she works so hard that it's not surprising. If you want to go up to bed, Anna, don't mind me. I'm a night owl. I'm never in bed before the early hours of the morning.'

Now surely Drewe would say something since Althea's determination to get him to herself couldn't have been more blatant, but he made no comment at all and Anna couldn't bear the situation any longer. She didn't intend to fight over her rights so she said quietly: 'I am rather tired so I think I will go to bed. I'll see you in the morning, Althea. Good night, Drewe.'

He stood up. 'Good night, Anna.' He walked to the door and opened it for her, paused as if he intended to say something, then thought better of it as she left the room.

Anna spent a wretched night. She couldn't banish Althea's triumphant face from her mind; it seemed to leer at her from every corner of the room. She'd thought she was in love with Ricky, but the pain she'd suffered when he married Sara was nothing compared with the anguish she was experiencing now. When she'd agreed to marry Drewe she'd told herself that she was doing it for Jeremy's sake, but that wasn't true. She did care for Jeremy and always would, but her overwhelming need was to be Drewe's wife and share her life with him.

She'd hoped Althea would breakfast

in bed but when she went into the dining-room Drewe and Althea were already there.

'It's a lovely morning,' said Althea, 'so I'm trying to persuade Drewe to come for a walk later on. Won't you join us, Anna?'

'I'd like to,' accepted Anna. 'I have some household shopping to do but I can easily postpone that until this afternoon.'

She was rewarded by the flash of anger in Althea's eyes, but the other girl recovered immediately.

'Good,' she cried. 'I know Sara keeps some walking shoes here so I'll borrow them since we take the same size. Where shall we go, Drewe? You know all the best routes.'

'Through the woods and over the fields,' he suggested. 'I'll join you in about half an hour. I've a couple of telephone calls to make before I go out.'

'And I must look in on Sara,' remarked Anna.

'I've already seen her,' said Althea.

'She had a fairly good night considering everything, but she's having breakfast in bed. Mrs. Mabledon's taking it up to her.'

By her attitude she might have been in sole charge of the household, but because she was a guest Anna tried not to show her resentment. It made her determined, however, to challenge Althea for Drewe's attention so she made up her face with extra care and put on a new dark green sweater with her camel coloured trouser suit.

Sara was sitting up in bed, languidly drinking coffee and crumbling a piece of toast.

'How do you feel this morning?' asked Anna.

Sara shrugged. 'How do you expect anyone to feel who's been deserted by her husband? Naturally you'll be glad it's happened because you consider I stole Ricky from you, but even if he hadn't met me he'd never have married you.'

'No, perhaps not,' agreed Anna

calmly, 'and although you may find this difficult to believe it doesn't give me the slightest pang. I once thought I was in love with him, but I realised some time ago that my feelings for him had changed.'

'It's all very well to say that now,' scoffed Sara, but there was a note of uncertainty in her voice.

'Shall I take your tray?'

'You might as well. I don't feel like getting up yet so I'm going to doze again.'

She lay back on her pillows, and Anna pulled the blankets round her. Sara seemed surprised but closed her eyes while Anna walked quietly out of the room.

She had to admit that she didn't really enjoy the walk through the woods and across the fields. She had the satisfaction of knowing that she'd prevented Althea from being alone with Drewe, but she couldn't derive much comfort from that. He divided his conversation impartially between them, but all the time Anna felt herself an intruder and she was glad to have the excuse of the household shopping to take her out after lunch.

Occambridge was crowded, and she was pushed and jostled as she made her way from one shop to the other. She longed for a cup of tea but all the cafés were full and it seemed better to wait until she reached home. She drove back to Heathlands, and went in by way of the kitchen to dump her parcels. Mrs. Mabledon was out so Anna switched on the kettle and walked through to the drawing-room to see what the others were doing. The door was slightly open, and before she entered the room she could see a cosy intimate picture of two people having tea together.

Althea was leaning forward as she poured out, and Drewe was laughing at something she said. Anna stood still for a moment and then moved silently away, back to the kitchen where she made her tea and sat down at the table to drink it. What was she to do? Should she ask Drewe right out whether he still loved Althea or should she swallow her pride and remain silent?

She buried her face in her hands until with the rattle of a trolley at the door she jerked herself upright. Althea came in with the tea things, saying: 'When you didn't return I thought I'd better make tea for Drewe and myself.'

'I'm sorry to be late,' said Anna mechanically. 'There was so much traffic in Occambridge I couldn't get along very quickly.'

Althea surveyed her mockingly. 'And I don't suppose you exactly hurried back. You're not a fool, you can see the way things are going.'

'I don't know what you mean.'

'Oh, my dear, you don't need to pretend with me. I've known Drewe longer than you have, and it's quite obvious he regrets having asked you to marry him. He proposed on the rebound after our stupid quarrel, but he's too honourable to ask you to release him. That will be up to you.'

'But suppose I don't want to break our engagement?' said Anna desperately.

'What kind of a marriage do you think you'll have if you hold him to it? Do you believe it could possibly be a success when all the time you would be aware that he'd only married you out of a sense of duty?'

Anna couldn't speak, and after a moment Althea went on persuasively: 'There's really only one course for you to take and if you're sensible you'll admit it — tell Drewe that you can't marry him after all and go away.'

8

'But I can't do that,' protested Anna, desperately clutching at any excuse. 'There's Sara to be looked after. She isn't fit to go back to the flat, and Mrs. Mabledon couldn't be expected to cope with everything.'

'She wouldn't need to. I'd stay on here until Sara was better and something had been resolved between her and Ricky. Drewe's going up to London on Monday to talk to Ricky and find out what the situation is. That's another thing. If you remove yourself from the scene Sara will soon come round, and in a few days she and Ricky will be together again. You must see that your absence would solve a lot of problems.'

'Yes, I admit that,' said Anna dully. 'Very well, I'll go.'

'You're doing the right thing,' and triumphantly Althea went away.

Anna sat there in a stupor of misery until Mrs. Mabledon returned. The housekeeper took one look at her and exclaimed: 'Mercy on us, what's happened? You look dreadful.'

'It's only a headache,' lied Anna. 'I made myself a cup of tea but it hasn't cured it.'

'If I were you I should lie down for a while.'

'I think I will.'

Anna went up to her room to think but at the end of an hour she was merely back at the same point, the admission that her disappearance from the scene would be best for everyone. Best for everyone but herself and Jeremy that was, and even he, with the distraction of school, would soon forget her. At least she hoped so because she loved him but not, she realised, as much as Drewe. Because she cared so deeply for Drewe his happiness came before everything, and if this depended on his marrying Althea then he must be free to do it.

Anna having finally decided this it only remained to work out a plan. She would have to go away without telling him in advance, otherwise she didn't think she would have the resolution to carry things through. Althea had said that Drewe was going up to London on Monday to seek out Ricky so that would be her opportunity to slip away. She would go to Cornwall. At this time of the year the hotel would certainly be able to accommodate her but to make doubly sure she would walk down to the call box at the crossroads this evening and telephone to Mrs. Brayle.

Sara decided to get up for dinner, and since attention was focused on her when she came down Anna seized the opportunity to slip down to the telephone box. Mrs. Brayle sounded delighted to hear from her, and assured her that she could have a room if she came down on the Monday.

'Is it a short holiday?' she asked, 'or are you leaving Sussex? If so you can have your old job back any time you like. I missed you a lot this summer. The receptionist I engaged wasn't nearly so efficient.'

'I'm leaving this job but I don't quite know what my future plans are,' said Anna evasively. 'I thought I'd have a rest before deciding what to do next.'

'Very sensible, and we can have a good talk when you get here. I'll expect you on Monday.'

Now that that was settled Anna felt both better and worse. She walked slowly back to Heathlands, hoping to be able to enter the house unobserved, but to her dismay as she made her way up the drive Drewe came out. His brows drew together in a frown.

'Where have you been?' he demanded. 'I've been looking for you.'

'I had a headache. I thought the fresh air would help me to get rid of it.'

'On a cold February evening? Look, you and I never seem to get a moment alone with one thing and another but I must talk to you. Nothing's worked out as I thought it would and I realise that's my fault, but now, confound it, Sara's here and Althea too which is another complication.'

'I know,' said Anna quickly, 'but I do understand the situation and it will all come right.'

His gaze was searching. 'You mean that, Anna? You'll be happy?'

Tears that she was forcing back were stinging her eyes. 'I've worked things out; I know what I'm doing,' she babbled. 'I — I must get a handkerchief. I think I'm starting to get a cold.'

She pushed past him because she couldn't bear any more and had to get away. He'd obviously realised that things couldn't go on as they were, that he ought to tell her he still loved Althea. Well, she would save him the trouble; she thought he would be grateful to her for that.

All the next day she avoided him which wasn't difficult since Althea monopolised him. Anna was left to attend to Sara who was in a restless, nervous state. She came down after having breakfast in bed and wandered aimlessly round the house, following Anna wherever she went. Anna was surprised at this, expecting Sara to cling to Althea, but instead the two of them kept apart. After lunch Drewe retired to his study to look at some papers while Althea yawned as she flicked through a magazine.

'This is deadly,' she remarked. 'I shall go mad if I sit here any longer so I'm going out in the car. Do you want to come, Sara?'

'No,' answered Sara quickly. 'I don't feel like going out today.'

'It would be far better for you than brooding here, but it's up to you. See you at dinner.'

She sauntered out, and Sara glanced furtively at Anna.

'I thought — well, it's possible that Ricky might ring me,' she said aggressively.

'Quite possible,' Anna agreed.

She returned to the book she was reading and suddenly Sara asked in a much more subdued tone: 'Do you think he will? I — I suppose you think I shouldn't have said what I did to him, but he infuriated me meeting you secretly and coming down here behind my back.'

Anna laid down her book. 'Sara, you and Ricky will have to work things out for yourselves, but I repeat that you've nothing to fear from me. The feeling Ricky and I had for each other vanished long ago.'

'But I taunted him with wishing he'd married you. I accused him of having married me for my money.'

Looking back Anna believed that the money had influenced Ricky to propose to Sara, but there was no point in admitting it. Sara needed reassurance now. Anna guessed that she genuinely cared for Ricky, and was afraid that by her taunts she'd lost him for ever.

She said gently: 'You do love him, don't you?'

'Yes, I do,' whispered Sara. 'Only since we've been married I've been afraid that he didn't love me. It's made me bad-tempered and careless so that I didn't bother to cook or shop properly. Now we're going to have a baby and we didn't plan to start a family so soon. I'm afraid Ricky will be furious and blame me for it.'

'He can't do that, it's as much his fault as yours,' pointed out Anna briskly. 'I don't want to hand out advice, Sara, but if I were you I'd tell him that I was sorry for what I'd said and suggest you both made a fresh start. I'm sure you'll find him ready to agree.'

'Do — do you really think he will?'

'Yes,' said Anna with firm conviction.

She knew Ricky. With his tendency to take the easy way out and his hatred of scenes she was sure that after a token resistance he'd make it up with Sara. If he had really married her for her money at the same time he'd been attracted to her, and there was no reason why they shouldn't settle down to an amiable existence if Sara weren't too demanding. Anna could see now that Ricky would never fall desperately in love with anyone. What he chiefly asked from life was comfort and security, and he would be prepared to stay with any woman who could provide them.

'But there's been no word from him.'

'I expect he considers himself very much the injured party, but Drewe's going up to London tomorrow, isn't he, to investigate matters? If you make it clear to him that you're willing to go halfway towards a reconciliation I don't think he'll have any difficulty in persuading Ricky to agree.'

Sara immediately looked a great deal more cheerful and said: 'My hair looks terrible. I wish I could wash it so that if Ricky should come down with Drewe — '

'The doctor wanted you to rest so I don't think you ought to tire yourself, but we could make your hair more presentable by using a dry shampoo. Shall I try it for you?'

Sara agreed eagerly, and was pleased with the result. Afterwards she decided to lie down until dinner, and Anna took the opportunity to pack her cases. She also attempted to compose a letter to Drewe, but it proved very difficult to write. In the end she made it as brief as possible, telling him simply that she thought she was taking the least embarrassing way out for both of them. She couldn't help adding that she'd loved living at Heathlands and that she was sorry to let Jeremy down but hoped he would forgive her. Then she put the note in her handbag ready to leave out for Drewe after he had gone up to London the next day, and went down to dinner.

Sara, her hair shining and her face carefully made up, was quite animated at dinner, and suggested to Drewe that he should take her up to London with him the next day.

'No,' he said firmly. 'After all this upset you're staying here until this affair's properly sorted out. I don't want a repetition in a week or two. I've my own plans to formulate.'

'Of course. I'd forgotten you're getting married at Easter.' Sara shot an apologetic glance at Anna.

'Exactly,' replied Drewe grimly, and Althea interposed smoothly: 'Drewe, would it be putting you out if I didn't go back to town tonight but stayed until tomorrow? Traffic's always so heavy on a Sunday evening.'

'Stay by all means until tomorrow,' agreed Drewe, but just for a moment Anna could have sworn that there was disappointment in his eyes. Obviously she must be mistaken since he would be only too glad for Althea to stay on. Anna had to admire her skill in ensuring that she would be here when he came home the following evening. She certainly had a knack of twisting events to her advantage.

So when Sara retired early to bed there was no question of Anna and Drewe being left alone together. Althea stayed with them, talking in a lively fashion, and Anna was glad of it. She could only keep up her resolution to leave Heathlands the next day by reminding herself how much Althea meant to Drewe. Out of politeness he tried to draw her into the conversation several times, but each time Althea switched it back to a more intimate level. Finally the strain became too much for Anna so she announced that she was going to bed and said goodnight before either of the other two could demur. Not that she expected any protests since Althea at least would be only too glad for her to disappear, but she thought that perhaps Drewe felt guilty at the way he was neglecting her. Well, after tomorrow he needn't think about her again which would be a relief to him.

She undressed and got into bed but she couldn't sleep. Images of all the events of the past few months crowded into her mind and wouldn't be banished. She would never forget the summer which had just gone — the shape and feel of it. It was difficult to realise that she'd once disliked Drewe, but it would have been better if she'd never fallen in love with him and had been spared the dreadful pain of having to give him up. As she tossed restlessly the clock in the drawing-room faintly chimed first one then two, and she could bear it no longer. She didn't possess any sleeping tablets, but perhaps if she drank a glass of hot milk with two aspirins it would settle her nerves.

Creeping silently downstairs she went to the kitchen and put milk onto heat. As she turned to take a glass from the cupboard the kitchen door opened and Drewe stood there in dressing gown and pyjamas.

'I thought I heard a noise,' he said, 'so I came down to investigate.'

'I'm sorry,' faltered Anna. 'I didn't mean to disturb anyone but I couldn't sleep so I thought I'd heat some milk in the hope that it would send me off.'

'I couldn't sleep either,' he said

abruptly, and they stood staring at each other, Anna very conscious of her ruffled hair and filmy nylon negligée.

The milk boiled up suddenly, and Drewe stepped forward to grab the pan at the same moment as Anna reached for it. They collided, their bodies coming up hard against each other, and somehow as he thrust the pan to one side his other arm encircled Anna and he gave a half sigh, half groan. The next instant they were locked together in a long, despairing kiss.

For a brief moment Anna surrendered to the bittersweet ecstasy of Drewe's mouth on hers, then in a torrent of pain she thrust him away and fled for the stairs. She daren't let him touch her again or all her resolution would be undermined. She closed her bedroom door and locked it, then sank trembling onto her bed. If Drewe had knocked she didn't know what she would have done, but he didn't. She sat there, her heart beating wildly for ten long minutes, then she heard him come quietly upstairs and pass along the landing to his own bedroom. Not until then did she get into bed and lie there staring into the darkness until she fell at last into a half doze.

Once more Althea was down to breakfast, determined, Anna thought ironically, not to give her the chance of a last word with Drewe. Not that she had any intention of seeking one. This morning she felt lifeless, utterly drained of emotion. There was a letter in the post for her from Jeremy but she slipped it into her handbag to read later. She wanted to remain numb until she'd left the house, and when Drewe came out of the study with his brief-case she tensed herself.

He bent his head to brush her cheek conventionally with his lips, and when she flinched he said sombrely: 'I'll be back as soon as I can. You and I must talk; we can't go on like this. Last night — '

'There's no need to explain. We were both in an emotional state. It didn't mean anything.'

'Is that how you see it? I wondered — '

He broke off as Althea walked into the hall.

'Are you off, Drewe?' she asked brightly. 'Thank you for my nice weekend. I hope you have a successful interview with Ricky, but I don't think there's much doubt of that. Sara seems willing to play her part in a reconciliation which gives you an advantage.'

'Yes,' he agreed, turning to the front door and then looking back over his shoulder at Anna almost as if he were reluctant to leave. She forced herself to stay where she was and the next moment he'd gone, his car roaring down the drive.

Althea looked at her appraisingly. 'You haven't changed your mind?'

'No, I'm going this morning.'

'You haven't told Drewe?'

'I'm leaving a note for him.'

'Good. I think you're sensible to make a clean break now, and I'm sure

Drewe will be grateful to you. Men hate fuss and farewell scenes.'

Anna couldn't resist saying : 'You should know,' but the thrust had no effect on Althea.

'I'll run you to the station,' she offered.

Anna shook her head. 'No, thank you, I prefer to telephone for a taxi.'

Althea shrugged. 'Just as you wish. What about Mrs. Mabledon?'

'I'll see her before I go.'

Anna brought her cases into the hall, and then rang for a taxi. Mrs. Mabledon was in the kitchen checking the contents of the store cupboard, and turned to say: 'We'd better be ordering some more black cherry jam. Mr. Drewe's very fond of it, and I've opened the last jar. I'll put it on the shopping list if you're going into Occambridge this morning.'

'I'm not,' said Anna. 'Mrs. Mabledon, I'm leaving Heathlands. I'm going back to Cornwall.'

The housekeeper stared at her. 'Now?'

'Yes, my taxi will be here at any moment.'

'But I don't understand. Mr. Drewe said nothing to me.'

'He doesn't know, but I've left a letter for him on the dining-room mantelpiece. Will you see that he gets it?'

There was a ring at the front door.

'That will be my taxi,' said Anna. 'Goodbye, Mrs. Mabledon and thank you for all your help.'

'Wait,' cried the housekeeper urgently, but Anna fled into the hall before her courage should fail her. Althea was already instructing the driver to put her cases into the taxi and Anna leaped in after them, slamming the door.

'Occambridge station,' she said, 'and please hurry.'

The long journey to Cornwall unfortunately gave her time to think, and by the time she reached the Ocean Hotel she was weary both in mind and body. Mrs. Brayle took one look at her, then said: 'A light meal for you and bed.

We'll talk in the morning.'

Anna was only too thankful to obey, and rather to her surprise fell heavily asleep almost at once. She didn't wake until Mrs. Brayle tapped on her door the next morning with a breakfast tray, then she sat up, conscience-stricken.

'What time is it?' she asked. 'You shouldn't be waiting on me like this. You have enough to do.'

'You're a guest at the moment,' said Mrs. Brayle comfortably, 'and we haven't any other visitors. Besides, I wanted a word with you in private. What's brought you here so suddenly or would you rather not talk about it? If so, tell me to mind my own business.'

'There's nothing to tell except that I made a mess of things. Drewe Chatham and I decided to get married to give a settled home to Jeremy, and then Drewe discovered that he was still in love with his former fiancée so the easiest way out was for me to break the engagement and leave Heathlands.'

'You mean that he isn't in love with

you but you are with him,' speculated Mrs. Brayle shrewdly.

'Is it so obvious?'

'Only to someone who knows you very well. It's your affair, Anna, so I won't say anything more except that you're welcome to stay here as long as you like and slip back into your old job if that suits you. Think about it; don't decide at once.'

'Thank you. I would like a few days to sort things out in my mind.'

When Mrs. Brayle had gone downstairs Anna dressed and decided to unpack her things properly. Rummaging in her handbag for her keys she came across the unopened letter from Jeremy which she'd stuffed in yesterday morning, and sat down on the bed to read it. He told her that he'd gone up two places in form, that he might be chosen for the house hockey team, and reminded her that it was his exeat next Saturday and that she'd promised to come with Drewe to take him out to lunch.

She read that sentence over again with dismay. In the strain of the last few days she'd forgotten all about Jeremy's exeat. Now she would have to write and tell him that she wasn't coming. It wouldn't be fair to let him expect her and leave the burden of his disappointment to be borne by Drewe. There was no point in putting off the unpleasant task so she scribbled a letter immediately, explaining that she and Drewe wouldn't be getting married after all and that she had left Heathlands. It was impossible to go into details so she made the letter as brief as possible, the tears stinging her eyes as she imagined Jeremy's bewilderment when he read it. She prayed that he would soon forget her and that Althea would be kind to him, and then she sealed the envelope and went out to post it.

The next two days were fortunately fine, and she spent most of her time taking long walks and thinking about her future. There had been no sign from

Drewe and she didn't expect one. In her farewell letter she'd said merely that she was returning to Cornwall, but he must have guessed that she would go to the Ocean Hotel and the fact that he hadn't rung up to find out if she were there was an indication that he had accepted her gesture. By Thursday she'd made up her mind to leave the hotel at the weekend and look for another job. She would cut her losses entirely, sell the cottage when it became vacant again, and build her life afresh in new surroundings.

'I'll go up to London on Monday, find myself some accommodation, and register with an employment agency I know of in the Strand,' she told Mrs. Brayle.

'Though for my own sake I'd like you to stay on I think you've made a wise decision,' said Mrs. Brayle. 'There are too many memories for you down here.'

Anna had just sat down to dinner that evening when the hall porter, who doubled as odd-job man out of season, told her that there was someone asking for her.

'It's a boy, Miss,' he said, 'come up from Polcaster station in a taxi and got no money to pay the fare. He says to tell you it's Jeremy.'

Jeremy? What was he doing here? Leaving her soup Anna ran through the hall to where a forlorn figure stood in the foyer, a taxi-driver behind him.

'Here, what about my fare?' demanded the man aggressively. 'I haven't got all night to hang about. I only brought the lad out as a favour because I didn't want to see him stranded at the station.'

'I'm very grateful to you,' said Anna. 'How much do I owe you?'

She paid the man, adding a generous tip, and then turned to Jeremy.

'I'm sorry, Anna,' he gulped, 'but I was so hungry I had to buy some sandwiches on the train and then I didn't have enough money for a taxi.'

'That doesn't matter, but what are

you doing here? Have you run away from school?'

'I had to. You said you weren't coming over on Saturday, you said you weren't going to marry Drewe and live with us. Why aren't you? Won't I ever see you again?'

'Jeremy, listen to me.' She took his arm gently. 'Did you leave a note at school to say where you were going?'

'No, I was afraid that if I did they'd be able to stop me. I'd saved the money you and Drewe gave me when I went back to school and I borrowed some off Bates Minor and Phelps and it was just enough for a ticket to the station at Polcaster. Phelps told me that the trains to Cornwall went from Paddington, and when I got there they told me where to change.'

'You do see, don't you, that I must let them know you're here. They'll be frantic with worry, and by now the school has almost certainly got in touch with Drewe. Perhaps it would be better if I rang him.'

'I'll go back if you'll take me,' cried Jeremy. 'If you'll promise me to marry Drewe and live at Heathlands with us like you said you were going to.'

'I can't do that. Look, you must be hungry. Go and wash yourself in the downstairs cloakroom and I'll tell Mrs. Brayle that you're going to have dinner with me. While we're eating I'll explain why I can't go back to Heathlands.'

'I'm not hungry,' muttered Jeremy, but he went obediently to the cloakroom. Her heart aching for him Anna went in search of Mrs. Brayle and explained the situation briefly to her.

'Poor lamb,' said Mrs. Brayle sympathetically. 'It's hard on him but it can't be helped. I'll keep my eye on him while you telephone to Mr. Chatham.'

Anna braced herself to ring the Heathlands number. She longed yet feared to hear Drewe's voice again, and half hoped that he wouldn't be there so that she could leave a message with Mrs. Mabledon. He answered the telephone himself, however, and the familiar curt tone turned her knees to water.

'It's Anna,' she blurted out. 'I'm at the Ocean Hotel at St. Aurryns and Jeremy's just turned up here. It may be partly my fault for writing to him to explain that I couldn't go with you to the school this weekend, but I'd no idea that he would run away to see me.'

'Thank God he's safe. I had the school on earlier today to say that he was missing and that they were in touch with the police. Can you keep him overnight if I collect him tomorrow . . . '

'Yes, of course. Drewe, I'm sorry . . . '

'There's no need to be. It was an intolerable situation, much more my fault than yours, and you were right to take the sensible way out. I'm only sorry that you've had this trouble with Jeremy, but as soon as I pick him up you can put us all out of your mind for good.'

'Yes, of course,' she repeated, because there didn't seem anything else to say.

'Until tomorrow then.'

She needn't have feared speaking to him again. Obviously he'd been only too glad for her to take matters into her own hands judging by his business-like and impersonal manner. She went in search of Jeremy to do what she could to comfort him and found him in the dining-room, his face set and miserable.

She thought it would be easier to talk to him while they were eating, and he pushed his food round his plate as he listened to her careful explanation of why she had to leave Heathlands.

'But I don't understand,' he burst out. 'You said at Christmas you were going to marry Drewe. Why did you say it if it wasn't true?'

Anna hesitated. She hadn't meant to mention Althea but it looked as if she would have to do that to convince Jeremy that Drewe didn't want to marry her now. She began again.

'It's like this, Jeremy. You remember Drewe was going to marry Althea, then they had a quarrel and the engagement was broken off. A little while after that Drewe asked me to marry him and look after you for always because he knew I was happy at Heathlands, and I said yes. But it's very easy to make a mistake, and later on Drewe discovered that he still loved Althea so you see he and I wouldn't have been happy together. You can't make a success of marriage with one person if all the time you wish you were married to someone else.'

'But you wouldn't have wished you were married to someone else, would you?' persisted Jeremy.

Anna couldn't bring herself to lie to him. 'No, I wouldn't but that isn't enough. Both of you have to want to be married to each other.'

She was afraid she hadn't put it very clearly, but this time Jeremy seemed to understand. He sighed heavily.

'I see, but I wish it wasn't like that. Won't I ever be able to see you again, Anna?'

'Darling, I don't know. It might be

too difficult, but Althea will be kind to you.'

'She won't be like you,' said Jeremy desolately, and Anna got up from the table to put her arms round him.

'Things will be a lot better than you think, I'm sure of that. What would you like to do now? Play a card game?'

He was very subdued for the rest of the evening, but he seemed resigned to the future and made no fuss when it was time to go to bed. Anna felt wretchedly miserable and hoped that Drewe wouldn't be delayed. She and Jeremy went on the beach after breakfast the next morning and he told her the latest developments at school, insisting that he was going to write to her. She didn't try to dissuade him, certain that with so many other distractions his letters would soon cease.

Drewe arrived after lunch, having made an early start. From the lounge window Anna saw his car draw up and her mind went back to that summer day last year when she'd seen him for the first time. He walked towards the hotel with his rapid, easy stride, and she said to Jeremy: 'Here's Drewe. Let's go to meet him.'

Drewe was unsmiling, and though Anna couldn't wonder at it she sensed that it increased Jeremy's nervousness. It was difficult to think of something to say to ease the tension; it would be ridiculous to enquire whether he'd had a good journey. However, before she could dredge up some harmless remark Drewe said tautly: 'I hope you realise how much trouble you've put me to by this idiotic behaviour, Jeremy. I haven't any more time to waste so we'll start back right away.'

'Won't you have a short rest first?' suggested Anna impulsively. 'Jeremy, would you ask Mrs. Brayle if we could have a pot of coffee in the lounge?'

When he'd gone she turned back to Drewe.

'How is Sara?'

'Practically recovered as far as I can

tell. She and Beeston have decided to make a fresh start so let's hope things go smoothly from now on. I need to devote some time to my own affairs without these constant interruptions.'

'It was stupid of me to bring you all this way. Once I'd told you that Jeremy was safe there was no reason why I shouldn't have taken him back to school myself.'

'And no reason why you should. He's my responsibility not yours.'

'He wrote to me, you see, expecting me to go down to the school with you this weekend. I had to let him know that I wouldn't be there but I never anticipated his taking matters into his own hands.'

'No.'

Wasn't he going to help her at all? His face was rigid and his mouth grim. Surely he was relieved that she'd released him from their engagement? She'd expected him to be annoyed with Jeremy but not to be confronted with this stony unapproachability, almost as if he were furious with her too.

She said hesitatingly: 'My note — I thought it would be less embarrassing for you if I left without seeing you again.'

'And for you too, under the circumstances. I agree the situation had become intolerable as it was and I intended us to have a frank discussion as soon as Althea had gone, but since you felt you couldn't wait for that you did the best thing.'

'It wasn't so much that I couldn't wait,' began Anna, 'as that — ' but at that moment Jeremy appeared carrying a tray with cups and saucers and a coffee pot.

'Mrs. Brayle said I could bring it myself,' he announced. 'May I have a cup of coffee, Anna?'

She poured him a cup of milky coffee, wishing that he hadn't interrupted them at that precise moment. There was no chance for her to have any further private conversation with

Drewe because he drank his coffee quickly and then rose, impatient to be on his way. She didn't seek to detain him any longer but said goodbye to Jeremy as cheerfully as she could. As he hugged her his lips trembled but he didn't cry.

Drewe put his hand on the boy's shoulder as he said: 'Goodbye, Anna. Don't blame yourself. I should never have persuaded you into that engagement but I'd hoped . . . '

She saw a muscle twitching at the side of his jaw and for one incredible moment she thought he was going to reach out and take her into his arms. It was as if her breath stopped, but the next moment he turned away, saying: 'Come along, Jeremy,' and they walked to the car. They got inside and the car began to move down the drive. She lifted a hand to Jeremy's frantic wave, the car gathered speed, swerved out of the gates, and was gone.

Anna stood quite still, staring unseeingly down the drive. She must have been mad to interpret that look on Drewe's face as one of longing, but what did he mean by saying that she wasn't to blame herself? Was it for disappointing Jeremy? Yes, that must be it. Now everything was finally over and she must forget the Chathams completely. On Monday she would go to London and try to fix herself up with a new job, if possible something demanding which would absorb all her time and energy.

Mrs. Brayle was in the lounge collecting the coffee cups.

'You'll feel better now they've gone,' she said. 'I suppose you wouldn't like to take the car into Polcaster and pick up some stuff for me? The shop can't deliver until tomorrow and I could really do with it tonight.'

'Yes, I'll do that.'

Anna suspected this was a contrived errand to occupy her for the rest of the afternoon, but she was too thankful to have something to do to question it. She pulled on a coat and drove into

Polcaster, picking up the carton of groceries for Mrs. Brayle and then sauntering round the market to end by browsing among the paperbacks in a bookshop. When she arrived back at the hotel she noticed a car parked in the drive, and after a second glance she blinked at it incredulously. It was Drewe's car, there was no mistaking the number, but what was it doing here when he should have been miles away by now?

She drove slowly round to the garage, trying to adjust to the idea of seeing him again. He must have had a puncture or a breakdown — no, because in that case he couldn't have reached here in his own car — surely Jeremy hadn't been taken ill — and then she stopped thinking altogether because he was coming towards her.

For a moment she was unable to say a word, then she gasped: 'What — ' but he didn't give her time to finish.

As she got out of the car he grasped her arm and said: 'You and I are going to have that talk after all. Come into the hotel.'

'But I don't understand. Why have you come back and where's Jeremy?'

'With Mrs. Brayle.'

Drewe marched her into the hotel and into the unoccupied dining-room.

'Mrs. Brayle assured me that we wouldn't be disturbed here so you can take your time but I want a straight answer. Why did you break our engagement?'

'I — I should have thought it was perfectly clear. Drewe, what is all this?'

'What is obvious to you may not be quite so obvious to me. I'm not exactly flattered that you could confide your reasons to Jeremy while leaving me to guess at them.'

'But you must have known that it was because I realised you were still in love with Althea. Jeremy would only confirm that.'

'On the contrary, Jeremy told me something which I didn't even suspect. I thought you couldn't forget Ricky

Beeston, and because of that found it impossible to face the prospect of marrying me. Darling heart, I don't know which of us has been the more stupid.'

'I — you can't mean — ' began Anna incoherently, but once again she wasn't allowed to finish her sentence. This time she was swept into Drewe's arms without any hesitation, and kissed with a thoroughness which left her dazed with disbelief that this could really be happening to her. At last he held her away from him and smiled tenderly down at her.

'Sit down and let's sort things out properly.'

'Yes,' agreed Anna weakly. 'I think that would be a good idea. Do you mean that you're not in love with Althea?'

'Just that. My disenchantment with Althea began when I realised that I didn't matter personally to her at all. I think originally it must have been the combination of sun and snow which blinded me to the fact that though she looked charming she was completely ruthless in getting her own way and considered no one but herself. You were quite different.'

'But you didn't approve of me at all when we met at the hotel and I didn't like you either.'

Drewe grinned. 'No, we certainly didn't fall in love at first sight, but as time went on I found myself revising my opinion of you so that when my engagement to Althea was broken I decided that though it was obvious you were in love with Beeston it could be possible for us to make a go of marriage if only for Jeremy's sake. It wasn't until I saw you again at Christmas that I discovered I was in love with you and that I couldn't bear you to disappear from my life.'

'But you were so matter of fact about our relationship that I didn't think you cared for me at all.'

'Because I felt I had to walk very warily. I believed you were still in love with Beeston, and even though he'd married Sara I thought that if I made any emotional demands on you you might take fright. I reasoned that my only hope lay in marrying you first and then wooing you afterwards when you'd had time to adjust to his loss.'

'I did think I was in love with Ricky,' acknowledged Anna, 'but I discovered some time ago that it couldn't have gone very deep because I couldn't stop thinking about you. When I believed that you were still in love with Althea I realised that what I'd felt for Ricky was nothing compared with my feeling for you, but I knew I couldn't hold you to our engagement if you cared for someone else. The least embarrassing way out for both of us seemed for me to disappear.'

'What made you so sure that I was still in love with Althea? Did she by any chance hint at it?'

'Yes, and when you invited her to stay and appeared to enjoy her company I didn't take much convincing.'

'I only issued that invitation because I felt under an obligation to her for bringing Sara down, but I was longing for her to go so that I could find out exactly how you felt about me. I could see that you weren't happy, but I hoped I could persuade you to marry me and let me take care of you. You seemed to hold aloof from me so that I was afraid of scaring you away completely if I made love to you as I wanted to do. The letter which you left for me was so cool and impersonal that I was convinced I must be abhorrent to you otherwise I would have got in touch with you as soon as I received it.'

'When you didn't I took it as proof that you were relieved at what I'd done.'

'Well, thank God Jeremy took it into his head to come here to you otherwise this muddle might never have been resolved. We hadn't gone very far today before he burst into tears and poured out everything you'd said to him with the result that I turned straight round and came back. That reminds me, I ought to ring the school and tell them that he won't be returning until tomorrow, but it can wait until I've kissed you again.'

At that moment Jeremy put his head round the door.

'I've had my tea,' he announced, 'so may I watch television until I go to bed?'

'You may do anything you like,' said Drewe recklessly, 'so long as you go away.'

'Why?' asked Jeremy with interest.

'Because I want to kiss Anna. Now scram.'

'He'll probably tell Mrs. Brayle exactly what you said,' murmured Anna, but as Drewe's mouth came down on hers again she knew she didn't care. Nothing at all mattered now that a lifetime together stretched before them.

Other titles in the Linford Romance Library:

YOUR SECRET SMILE

Suzanne Ross Jones

When Sean left town to go travelling, he took a piece of Grace's heart with him. It's taken years for her to get over him and at last she's reached a place where she's happy on her own. Her time is filled with good friends and fulfilling work as a maths teacher. But when Sean reappears as an art teacher at Grace's school, it's obvious he's intent on causing havoc in her well-ordered life.

ACCIDENT PRONE

Anna Ramsay

From hospital ward sister to sanatorium sister at Ditchingham Prep School is a drastic change, but Ruth Silke needs something different. Working with Dr Daniel Gather, the local GP who covers the school, isn't so easy — particularly when he seems all too matter-of-fact about his young son Danny, a boarder at the school. Ruth is convinced that Danny's accidents are a cry for help, but how to persuade Dan? Particularly when their own relationship leaves so much to be desired . . .